Edward Sims Van Zile

The Manhattaners

A Story of the Hour

Edward Sims Van Zile

The Manhattaners
A Story of the Hour

ISBN/EAN: 9783744747486

Printed in Europe, USA, Canada, Australia, Japan

Cover: Foto ©Andreas Hilbeck / pixelio.de

More available books at **www.hansebooks.com**

THE MANHATTANERS

A Story of the Hour

BY

EDWARD S. VAN ZILE

AUTHOR OF

"A MAGNETIC MAN," "LAST OF THE VAN SLACKS,"
ETC., ETC:

NEW YORK

LOVELL, CORYELL & COMPANY

1895

THE MANHATTANERS.

CHAPTER I.

"I DON'T want to discourage you, my boy, but, as our 'brevier writers' are so fond of saying, there is 'food for reflection' in that historic figure."

It was half an hour after midnight, and two men were standing at the south-west corner of City Hall park, gazing at the statue of Nathan Hale. The taller of the two was a man who, having passed the portentous age of forty, no longer referred to his birthday when he reached it. He had maintained silence on this subject for several years, and his friends were not certain whether he was forty-one or forty-five; but his face seemed to indicate the latter age. It was a strong face, marked with lines of care, perhaps of dissipation, and about the mouth lurked an expression of discontent. That he had grown rather weary of the battle of life was indicated by his dress, which possessed that indefinable characteristic that may be expressed as careless shabbiness. His beard was untrimmed, and a slouch hat covered a head of iron-gray hair that would have been picturesque had it not been constantly neglected.

His companion was a youth of not more than three-and-twenty, slender, carefully attired, and with a delicately-moulded face that was strikingly handsome when he smiled. He was showing his perfect teeth at this moment, as he glanced first at the statue of the martyred hero, and then at the sarcastic countenance of his companion.

"Why do you say that, Fenton? Surely there is inspiration in the sight. Does not the figure prove that the time-worn slur regarding the ingratitude of republics is false?"

"Hardly that, Richard — *Richard Cœur de Lion* I shall dub you for awhile. It simply shows that somebody, at a very late day, had an attack of spasmodic sentimentality. There

are other heroes of the Revolution, who were
as self-sacrificing and patriotic as Nathan Hale,
who are still forgotten by a republic that is
grateful only in spots.   Immortality, my dear
youngster, is, to a great extent, a matter of
chance.   But, to waive that point, don't you
see how this figure of enthusiastic youth, this
doomed martyr — this complete tie-up on Broadway, as a flippant friend of mine once called
the statue — illustrates the dangers that beset
your path?"

"I must acknowledge," answered Richard
Stoughton good-naturedly, as he placed his
arm in Fenton's and walked westward toward
the Sixth Avenue elevated station at Park
Place, "I must acknowledge that I have seen
nothing in the park that tended to dampen my
natural enthusiasm, unless it was the sign,
'Keep off the grass.'"

"That's just it," returned John Fenton in
his deep, penetrating voice. "That statue of
Nathan Hale is what might be called an emphasis in bronze of the warning, — a warning
as old as human tyranny, — to keep off the

grass. Hale failed to obey it, and went to an early death. Take warning, Richard, by the lesson the statue teaches. Don't let your dreamy and unpractical enthusiasm carry you into the enemy's camp. They'll hang you if you do."

"Your words are enigmatical," commented Stoughton, as the two men seated themselves in an elevated train bound up-town. "I had looked to you for comfort and warmth, and you give me a shower-bath."

"Poor boy!" smiled Fenton, less cynically than was his wont. "When did the youthful warrior ever gain anything of value by consulting the battle-scarred and defeated veteran? I have the decayed root of a conscience somewhere that troubles me now and then. It gave a little twinge just now, and causes me to doubt the wisdom and justice of my effort to open your eyes to the truth."

"But why," asked the younger man earnestly, "should there be anything to offend your conscience in telling me the truth?"

"Ah, there, my boy, you ask a question that

the wisest men have failed to answer. There are certain truths that the universe holds in its secret heart and refuses to divulge. As a microcosm, every man cherishes in his innermost being some bitter certainty that he must defend from the gaze of the curious. If he draws the veil, even by a hair's-breadth, that exposed nerve known as conscience will throb for an instant, and close his mouth."

"But," persisted the younger man, whose clear-cut face looked, in contrast with his companion's, like a delicate cameo beside a mediæval gargoyle, "I had placed so much value on your advice and sympathy."

"My sympathy you certainly have," said Fenton rather harshly; "but giving you my advice would be — to take a liberty with a time-honored illustration — like casting swine among pearls. Is it not some word-juggler, who uses epigrams to conceal the truth, who says that the only vice that does not cling to youth is advice?"

Richard Stoughton's face flushed, and his dark gray eyes glanced questioningly at his companion.

"I sometimes think," he said rather sadly, "that you are all brains and no heart, John Fenton."

"You are mistaken, my boy," answered Fenton quickly. "In that case I would have been a millionnaire long ago. I was afflicted with just enough heart to hamper my brain. The result is that I'm an assistant city editor in the prime of life, with a very short hill to roll down to the grave. But never mind what I am, or what I might have been. You are the only interesting personage present. You have come, like Nathan Hale, out of the 'Down East,' so to speak, to New York, to offer your youthful enthusiasm to a world that has too little of that sort of thing; so little, in fact, that it immortalizes Hale's sacrifice, and forgets his mission."

Fenton was silent for a moment.

"Just what do you mean by that last remark?" asked Richard gently.

"I mean that this great metropolitan community is suffering from a tyranny greater than that against which Hale and his contempo-

raries protested. I mean that we erect statues
to-day to lovers of liberty, to martyrs in the
cause of freedom, while we blindly and sub-
missively bow our heads to a yoke more tyrannical than that which the House of Hanover
held over our forefathers. I mean that Nathan
Hale died in vain, unless his example shall in-
spire a generation yet to come to rise against
an oppression more unjust, more pervasive, and
more impregnable than any the world has ever
seen."

Richard Stoughton looked at his companion
in amazement. Fenton's face was flushed, a
baleful light gleamed in his large, heavy eyes,
and he seemed to be talking more to himself
than to his companion. As they left the train
at Twenty-third Street and strolled eastward,
the elder of the two continued in a calmer
tone,—

"You haven't seen much of life, Stoughton.
You will find it necessary to repair, as rapidly
as possible, the intellectual ravages of a college
education. The tendency of Yale life is to
convince you at graduation that you know

everything. The experience of a few years in metropolitan newspaper life will convince you that you know nothing."

"And the last state of this man is happier than the first?" interrogated Richard lightly.

"Alas, my boy, I fear not. But perhaps that may be a local issue, a personal equation. I was more contented when I measured the circumference of knowledge by the diameter of my own experience than I am at present when I realize that what I know is so insignificant that it has no mathematical value at all. But my experience has no significance in connection with yours. The chances are that your career will be very different from mine. I certainly hope that it will be. At all events, you have the game to play, and the stakes are on the board. I drew to good cards, but somebody else won the pot. But what of it? There would be no fun in the game if everybody won and nobody lost."

Fenton smiled as he stopped in front of a brilliantly lighted saloon, and held out his hand to Richard Stoughton.

" Good-night, my boy, and good luck. I'll do what I can for you on the paper — and let me give you a word of advice, don't believe all I say. Somehow — and of course I'm sorry for it — I've got just a little romance left in my composition, the ruins of a magnificent air-castle I once built. It is sufficient for me to take an interest in the structure you're going to build on the firm foundation of youth, education, enthusiasm, and natural cleverness. I'll do what I can to add a stone now and then to your castle, my boy. And so, good-night."

The two men shook hands cordially, and Richard turned to hurry up-town to his rooms in Twenty-eighth Street, when Fenton called him back.

· " You understand, *Richard Cœur de Lion,* that it was not rudeness that prevented my asking you to join me in a drink. I was thinking of your castle, my boy. It'll tumble about your head if you put alcohol in the cellar. Good-night, old fellow. I must have some whiskey. Good-night."

CHAPTER II.

" THE Percy-Bartletts," as *Town Tattle* always called them in the weekly paragraph that
it devoted to their doings, were dining alone,
" en tête-à-tête and *en famille,"* as the husband
sometimes remarked in a mildly sarcastic way.
Not that Percy-Bartlett was in the habit of
being satirical. Far from it! He considered
sarcasm and satire the outward and visible —
or, rather, audible — sign of an inward and
hereditary tendency toward vulgarity. The
use of these weapons of speech implied that
one possessed both temper and originality —
characteristics that were not approved in the
set in which the Percy-Bartletts moved. But
Percy-Bartlett had, by inheritance, a rather
peppery disposition, and a mind naturally given
to creative effort. It was greatly to his credit,
therefore, that he had rubbed his manners and
speech into an almost angelic smoothness, and

had so thoroughly stunted such mental qualities as were not included in the accepted flora-
of-the-mind recognized by his set that he
passed current as a man in no danger of ever
saying or doing anything that would attract
special attention to him on the part of the
world at large. It is not generally known, but
it is nevertheless a fact, that it sometimes requires heroic self-restraint to become a " howling swell " — a vulgar term that cannot be
avoided by the writer in his effort to convey
to the reader the exact social status of Percy-
Bartlett. He was known to the lower orders
of society as a "howling swell," which means,
of course, that howling was the very last thing
in which he would indulge. There are those,
the poet tells us, who never sing, and die with
all their music in them. In like manner the
modern aristocrat is one who never howls, and
dies with all his howling in him.

Let it not be thought for a moment that the
perfect self-control exercised by Percy-Bartlett
indicated that there was nothing in his life to
try the temper of either a saint or a howling

swell. In fact, the temptation to give way to his hereditary testiness was with him, practically, at all times. Percy-Bartlett had nobly triumphed over all tendency toward originality. His wife had not. It was Mrs. Percy-Bartlett who constantly tried Percy-Bartlett's temper. If you are a married man, O reader, you will realize the full significance of the assertion, now made with due solemnity and emphasis, that, in spite of this fact, Mr. Percy-Bartlett had never said an unkind word to her, had never crossed her will, had never shown her, by word or deed, that he was bitterly disappointed at her refusal to walk in the very narrow path that society prescribed for her.

It must be acknowledged that there was something in the face and manner of Mrs. Percy-Bartlett that rendered her husband's hesitancy about opposing her will seemingly explicable. Her dark-brown eyes, golden-brownish hair, clear-cut nose and mouth, and perfect teeth combined to give her a beauty that won from every man a chivalric reverence

—from every man, that is, who is awed by the loving-kindness of the Creator in scattering flowers here and there in a weed-choked earth. Furthermore, there was something in Mrs. Percy-Bartlett's way of using her hands and moving her head that told of a will-power as highly developed as that which had enabled her husband to suppress every inclination to defy the pattern that had been adopted by his set. Percy-Bartlett had used his self-command to destroy originality. Mrs. Percy-Bartlett had made her will-power an ally of her creative genius. The outlook for a permanent peace between them was not bright, but we find them at dinner at a time when the *modus vivendi* was still in comfortable operation.

"And who sings for you to-night?" asked Percy-Bartlett, his calm, blue eyes resting on his wife coldly. He was a man of thirty-eight, with pale cheeks, thin lips, and immobile countenance. The fifteen years' difference in the ages of husband and wife was more than borne out by their faces. She looked younger than her years; he was younger than he looked.

"I think," she answered, "that it will be a great success. The new boy-soprano who has made such a sensation at St. George's is coming. So is Gordon Mackey, the tenor — you met him one night, you remember. Then Bryant Stanton is to play the 'cello, and Mlle. de Sarçon has promised to sing some of the 'Falstaff' music. Several others of less importance will be here, — Barton, the baritone, Miss Ely, the contralto, and so forth. Barton, you know, has been singing my cradle-song at his concerts."

Percy-Bartlett looked at his wife in a way that was distinctly unsympathetic. He seemed to be thinking that a cradle-song was something of a *tour-de-force* for a childless woman; but there are many things about a musical genius that a layman cannot hope to understand. Percy-Bartlett had learned his limitations in this direction long ago, and never asked his wife how or why she wrote vocal music that was slowly but surely gaining popularity. It was a cross he had to bear, and, like a perfect gentleman, he bore it in silence.

"Don't you think, my dear," suggested Mrs. Percy-Bartlett sweetly, as they arose from the table, "that you could endure just one evening of really good music?"

"You will have to let me off to-night, Harriet," answered Percy-Bartlett coldly. "I have a committee meeting at the club. By the way," he remarked as they entered the library, in the intellectual atmosphere of which he was in the habit of smoking his after-dinner cigar, "I had a letter to-day from a business friend of mine, a distant relative on my mother's side, Samuel Stoughton of Norwich. He tells me that his son, Richard, who was graduated from Yale last year, has come to the city to take a place on the *Morning Trumpet*. He asks me to show him a little attention. And, really, I don't see how I can get out of it."

"Why should you want to?" asked Mrs. Percy-Bartlett, striking a few chords on the piano, and casting a questioning glance at her husband. "The Stoughtons are very nice people."

"Oh, yes, of course. But then a newspaper

man, don't you know, may be all very well, but — really I can't understand why Richard Stoughton, who was left a fortune, if I remember rightly, by his mother, should take up the drudgery of New York newspaper life."

" Perhaps," suggested Mrs. Percy-Bartlett, looking down at her white, symmetrical arms and tapering hands, "perhaps the young man wants to see all sides of life. Perhaps he wants to enlarge his horizon."

"Humph," exclaimed Percy-Bartlett, showing more of his ancestral testiness than was his wont; "I can't understand such a motive. If running up and down the city until all hours of the night, making a nuisance of yourself, is enlarging one's horizon, I should think a man of Stoughton's position and education would prefer to remain narrow in his vision. But there is no accounting for tastes; and I must acknowledge that, of late years, a good many very nice fellows have gone into newspaper work. Well, we'll ask Stoughton to dinner some night when we're dining alone, and see what kind of a boy he is. Perhaps he'll get over his attack of journalistic enthusiasm as he recovered from the mumps or measles. His father has done me some good turns in business, and has it in his power to do more. I'll drop a note to Richard to-morrow and have him call at the office."

Percy-Bartlett threw away his cigar and rose to go. The picture his wife presented was irresistibly attractive. He bent over and kissed her. It was an unusual outbreak of emotion on his part, and Mrs. Percy-Bartlett smiled up at him as he turned to leave the room.

"How late," he asked as he reached the portière, "will your musical friends be here?"

"Oh, not late," she answered; "come home by twelve and you will find them gone."

.   .   .   .

The hour of midnight was striking.

"It was a great success, my little musicale," Mrs. Percy-Bartlett, with flushed, triumphant face, was saying to her husband as they stood in the drawing-room on his return. The evening had been a pleasant one to Percy-Bartlett, and the genial influences of his club had made him sociable.

"Come into the library, Harriet," he said, "while I smoke just one more cigar."

The smile on her face vanished, and lines of fatigue formed around her mouth.

"Please excuse me," she murmured in a weary tone. "I am very tired. They encored my cradle-song so many times that — that, really, it wearied me. I fear I can't stand success. Good-night. I'm very sorry."

"Good-night," he said coldly.

Then he went to the library and moodily lighted a "perfecto." There seemed to be something lacking in his life, something that forever seemed within his grasp and forever escaped him.

CHAPTER III.

"YES, Richard," remarked Fenton, as the two strangely-assorted newspaper men turned into a down-town side-street to take a *table d'hôte* dinner at a restaurant well known to the semi-Bohemians of the city, — real Bohemians we have none, though another generation will beget them, — "yes, my boy, this is the most interesting metropolis in the world."

He hesitated a moment, and taking Richard by the arm, stood still and looked about him at the passing throng.

"Within a radius of half a mile, Richard, not only every nation, but nearly every tribe, religion, sect, family, and name that the world has ever known has its representation. See, there's an Italian barber-shop across the street kept by a man named Cæsar. We are to dine at a French restaurant whose proprietor bears the historic family-name of Valois. I remem-

ber a few lines of an after-dinner poem one of
the men in the office read last year at a journalistic banquet.   It began : —

> " 'Did you say there was no romance
> In a town that deftly blends,
> In a picturesque mosaic,
> All the Old World's odds and ends ?
> In a city where the scapegoats
> Of the older countries meet,
> 'Tis a crazy-quilt of nations
> That is seen upon the street.' "

"It is, in a certain sense, the fact you have
just touched upon that brought me here," said
Richard, as they seated themselves at a small
table in a dining-room curiously decorated in
black and white.   Around them, seated in
small groups, were men whose faces bore the
European stamp.   Here and there a young
woman could be seen, smiling over her claret
at her *vis-a-vis*, her white teeth making her
dark eyes more striking by contrast.   There
was nothing distinctly American in the scene,
excepting a small, active, little newsboy, who
rushed from table to table selling the evening
edition of the *Trumpet*, and requesting patron-

age in a voice that indicated an ancestral brogue. Fenton, however, soon added one more native feature to the picture by ordering a Manhattan cocktail from a waiter who looked as though he might be a pretender to the throne of France, and sipping it slowly as he waited for Stoughton to explain himself.

"You see," went on the younger man, whose handsome face had already begun to attract the burning glances of several impressionable young women at the surrounding tables, "you see, I had my choice of going into the bank at Norwich, and depending upon my father's influence to push me forward in a line of life I detest, or coming to New York to follow my natural bent, and to broaden my views by contact with all kinds of people. Of course my father hoped that I would choose the former course. But how could I? How good this soup is, Fenton."

"Yes," answered the elderly journalist, who was much better groomed than the first time we met him; "the dinner they serve here is generally quite eatable—especially good, you know, if the proprietor realizes that you are a newspaper man. The next thing to being a millionnaire in New York, my boy, is to be a city editor." Fenton smiled in his usual sarcastic way.

"Then I go up a peg to-morrow night," remarked Richard playfully. "I dine with a city editor to-night, and with a millionnaire to-morrow night."

"Indeed." Fenton looked at his companion with an expression of interest on his face.

"Yes; I had a note a few days ago from a distant relative of my father's, Percy-Bartlett, who asked me to call on him at his office. He owns real estate, I think; but to judge from the number of his clerks, I don't think he can be overworked himself. At all events, he was quite cordial, in his touch-me-not kind of way, and I promised to dine with him and his wife to-morrow evening. I think he was astonished to find that I was no longer a reporter, for his cordiality increased when I told him about my promotion."

Fenton smiled rather coldly, and filled his glass with red wine.

"No wonder he was astonished, my boy," he said, as he set down his goblet; "I have been in active newspaper service for nearly fifteen years, and your elevation from the ranks is the most surprising occurrence in my recollection."

"I suppose it is remarkable," commented Richard, as the waiter served them with game that had been strong enough to break the law. "I haven't quite fathomed it myself."

"In one sense it is simple enough," continued Fenton. "'To him that hath shall be given,' you know, 'and to him that hath not,' etc. If you had been seeking a place as brevier writer or editorial paragrapher you could not have obtained it, but, presto, it comes to you unsought."

"Tell me all you know about it, Fenton," suggested the young man as he sipped his coffee.

"There is very little to tell," answered his companion as he lighted a cigar and gazed contentedly at the animated face before him. "A newspaper is an insatiable beast. Its maw is never satisfied. It swallows brains, talent, culture, industry, youth, maturity, wit, wisdom, with an appetite that grows with what it feeds upon. It is the hungriest monster the ages have produced, and its food is human lives."

"What an awful picture!" cried Richard cheerfully. "But what I am after is not the status of a newspaper in the cannibalistic realm, but the reason for my being given a desk in the editorial rooms."

"That's what I was coming to, Mr. Impatience. But you must let me get at it in my own way. Let me warn you against impetuosity, boy, and that awful affliction, vulgarly called 'the big head.' You have gone up like a rocket. You'll come down like a stick if you're not careful. And now, as to the cause of your rise. Know then, my young friend, that in the newspaper field men who can make epigrams are rare. Putting a column of fact into half an inch of fireworks requires a peculiar cast of mind. It may be said of paragraphers, as of poets, that they are born, not made. Now, without knowing it, you gave evidence in several of your news stories that you are the seventh son of a forty-second cousin, and can sound the well of truth with the plummet of a paradox. Mr. Robinson, who is an argus-eyed managing editor, if such a creature ever existed, was attracted by your sparkling generalizations, and made inquiries about you. He sent for me, and I told him that what his editorial page needed, above everything else, was a boy-paragrapher. And there you are."

Richard laughed. "I am exceedingly obliged to you, Fenton. I have noticed that calling a young man a boy is one of the favorite occupations of men of uncertain age."

"Well hit, Richard," cried the elder man, pushing one hand through his iron-gray locks, and motioning with the other to the waiter to refill his *liqueur* glass; "I like your — your 'spunk.' Isn't that what they call it 'Down East'? Another thing. You have given me a very conclusive proof that I am fond of you. My age, you know, is my sensitive spot. Isn't it curious that a man who prides himself on his devotion to pure reason, who glories in the fact that two and two make four, and whose life is

spent in the classification of facts, and the pre-
sentation of truth for the edification of the
public, should hesitate to acknowledge that he
was born on a certain date? Well, never mind!
Even the greatest men have flaws in their
make-up, Richard — and I have mine."

As they left the restaurant, strolling leis-
urely toward Broadway, they found the streets
less crowded than they had been an hour before.

"It is the time," said Fenton, " when the
city rests for a moment from labor, and pauses
to catch its breath before it begins to dissipate
— the interlude between its work for earthly
taskmasters and its work for Satan."

"What a cynic you are, Fenton!" exclaimed
Richard almost deprecatingly.

"Not at all, my boy. I will tell you what I
am some day. I am far from being a cynic;
but it makes me sad to think that this whole
fabric of society must undergo heroic treatment before any real progress in civilization
can be made."

"What do you mean?"

"I haven't time to explain just now. I will give you a few books to read, and your eyes may be opened to certain truths that will change your whole theory of life. It is seldom that I try to make a convert to my views, but I have observed surface indications on your part that you have brains. If you have, the time has come for you to learn that you live and move and have your being at a most critical time in the world's history. We are on the verge of great events, my boy, of great upheavals and vast changes. You will probably live to see them. I may or I may not. But whether I do or don't will make little difference to me, or to the world. But enough of this. I must get down to the office. And you, lucky man, have the evening to yourself. What will you do with it?"

"Go to hear the De Reszkes and Melba in 'Faust,' I think."

"Great scheme! It will do you good. It is much pleasanter watching Mephistopheles on the stage than fighting him in real life. I envy you, my boy. And to-morrow night you dine with a millionnaire. Be careful, Richard; remember Nathan Hale."

"I don't see the point," remarked the youth thoughtfully.

"I didn't think you would," answered Fenton; "but don't forget to come to me to-morrow for those books. I'll tell you at the same time what I know about the Percy-Bartletts, if you wish. Good-night."

Fenton boarded a cable-car going down town, and Richard Stoughton strolled moodily up Broadway.

"Fenton's a curious mixture," he muttered to himself. "I wonder what he was driving at."

CHAPTER IV.

"I FEAR," remarked Mrs. Percy-Bartlett, looking at Richard Stoughton with a pleased expression in her brown eyes, "that you studied the art of flattery at college and have not yet learned its worthlessness." She had been singing a little love-song that she had recently composed, and the thrilling melody had brought a flush of pleasure to the young man's face. Without knowing much about the science of music, he was keenly sensitive to its influence.

As he stood by the piano, looking down into the smiling face of the most beautiful woman he had ever met, Richard inwardly blessed the unexpected telegram that had called Percy-Bartlett away to his club before the coffee had been served at dinner. At the time of which we write, the financial affairs of the nation were in a disturbed state; and Percy-Bartlett, like other millionnaires, felt that a

great opportunity had presented itself to him
for combining patriotism and prudence, by giving aid to an improvident nation at a high rate
of interest.   His father had followed such a
course during the Civil War.   Percy-Bartlett's
financial patriotism was, as it were, hereditary,
and he had left the house that evening with
the firm determination of offering a tithe of
his fortune to his afflicted government, on gilt-
edged security, to be redeemed by posterity.

"You do me an injustice, Mrs. Percy-Bartlett," answered Richard, returning her smile.
"I know that my opinion regarding your song
is of no great value from a technical standpoint, but I can readily understand how glad
the publishers are to get your work."

Richard had learned much about the Percy-
Bartletts that afternoon from John Fenton.
He had heard of the husband's prominence
in society and business circles and in club
life, and of the wife's devotion to music, of
her talent as a song-writer.   But Fenton had
not told him that Mrs. Percy-Bartlett had
brown eyes that had a beseeching, almost

caressing expression at times, that her mouth
was rather large, but wonderfully symmetrical,
and especially attractive when she smiled and
showed her white, even teeth. Fenton had
been silent also regarding her brown hair —
hair that curled and shimmered and waved
with a coquettish life of its own, and gave to
Richard Stoughton an almost irresistible desire
to stroke it with his hand. That she had a
white, firm neck, and rounded, dimpled arms,
and long, tapering hands that were worthy a
sculptor's art, his friend had not informed him.
Perhaps Fenton did not know all this.

"At all events," thought Richard to himself,
"I'm inclined to think that if Fenton *could* see
her beauty, although he might admire it, he
would find some reason for saying that she
had no right to it — that so much of it as she
derived from her handsome ancestors was ill-
gotten gain." Which thought, the reader will
observe, proved that Richard had been skim-
ming the books Fenton had given to him, and
had come, as he fondly believed, upon certain
arguments that seemed to him to be founded

on fallacy. Stoughton never went very deeply into any subject presented to his attention. He had that faculty of mind which enabled him to cover a good deal of ground at a glance, and to condense into showy half-truths the results of his rapid mental processes. It was this gift — a dangerous one to a man who wishes to make a solid rather than a glittering success of life — that had suddenly given him a prominent place on the *Trumpet* as the spiciest paragrapher the editorial page had had for years. And it was this faculty applied to the airy nothings of unimportant conversation that had given him the reputation of being a wit — a reputation much more to be dreaded than that of a rake. No woman fears a rake, but she has a deep-seated dread of a wit.

"But come, Mr. Stoughton," said Mrs. Percy-Bartlett, standing up and looking at him with mock commiseration, "I have been very cruel to inflict my music on you, when I know that you are dying for a cigar. Come into the library and let me repair my lack of hospitality. Mr. Percy-Bartlett would feel that he had committed sacrilege if he failed to smoke a cigar after dinner."

"It would be something worse than sacrilege in such companionship," remarked Stoughton, lighting a "perfecto" and seating himself opposite his hostess; "it would be folly."

"There can be no folly, Mr. Stoughton, after marriage, you know. I mean in our set, of course. A thing is either good form or bad form. What is good form may seem foolish to the world at large, and what is bad form may, in reality, be wise. But our motto of *noblesse oblige* has absolutely nothing to do with folly or wisdom in the abstract. It simply presupposes an obligation on our part to observe certain canons of taste and habits of life that have no relation to wisdom or folly, virtue or vice, progress or retrogression. You know all this, though, as well as I do."

"Only in a general way," answered Richard, somewhat surprised at her earnestness. He felt that, somehow, she was tempted to treat him in a more confidential way than the duration of their acquaintanceship strictly warranted. "I have had little opportunity, as yet, to study the different phases of New York society."

"But," she persisted, her face slightly flushed with eagerness, "there is no difference in the social cult of the most exclusive set in New York and that which dominates the inner circle of other cities in what we might call the eastern belt of civilization. That awful Frankenstein called 'Bad Form,' a monster created by society, and dogging our steps at all times, is not confined to New York. Haven't you endured his threatening glances in your New England cities?"

"Yes," confessed Richard; "I know the creature — and, in a certain sense, I suppose I have run away from him. I came here to New York, against my father's wishes, that I might be free to live my life as my tastes and inclinations inspired me, not as a select few in my native city ordained that I should live it."

With an impetuous gesture Mrs. Percy-Bartlett placed her hand on his for an instant and blushed slightly as their eyes met.

"Do you know," she said, "I feel an almost irresistible inclination to tell you a secret, a secret that all the world knows, but that I have not yet confessed to a human soul." An odd smile played across her mouth.

"I shall feel more flattered than I can tell you," exclaimed Richard with marked emphasis.

"Well, then," went on Mrs. Percy-Bartlett, "I am a rebel. Remember, Mr. Stoughton, that this is the first time I have ever said this. I hardly know why I have said it to you; but, somehow, I feel thoroughly in touch with you on some points, and you seem more like an old friend than a new acquaintance."

Perhaps later on she would analyze this feeling more thoroughly, and realize that she had reached a crisis in her life when an attractive man in the first flush of youth, and still possessing a freshness of view, and the enthusiasm of newly tried powers that had already won recognition from the world, stimulated that part of her nature that the atmosphere in which she lived tended to repress. But, for the moment, she had not stopped to ask herself why Richard Stoughton attracted her. She had simply given herself up to the fascination he had for her, and had left to the future the solution of the problem as to how far she should allow this fascination to influence her.

"As a rebel," remarked Richard earnestly, "I give you greeting. I think I understand your revolt."

"I know you do," she exclaimed with enthusiasm. "You see, it is perfectly allowable for me to cultivate music as an accomplishment; but to take it seriously, to do something with it, to write songs that people outside of our circle will sing — that, you know, is bad form. I assure you, Mr. Stoughton, it took some courage to do it."

"But not to do it would have been a crime," said Richard, puffing his cigar thoughtfully.

"But a crime in the interest of the canons of good taste is not only allowable but imperative," returned Mrs. Percy-Bartlett, smiling. "You must understand that there is a vast difference between having your name in the newspapers as being one of the best-dressed women at the Patriarchs', and being referred to as a composer — both popular and promising."

"You mean that society would condemn you to die with all your music in you?"

"Practically, yes; but I refused to obey the sentence. Therefore, I am a rebel."

She arose, and he followed her into the music-room.

"Here's a little thing," she said, striking a few chords on the instrument, "that I have never sent to my publisher."

The chords ran into a weird, almost barbaric prelude. Then she began to sing. She had used the words of Heine's little gem of crystallized unrest : —

> "A pine-tree standeth lonely,
> On a far Norland height ;
> It slumbereth, while around it
> The snow falls thick and white.
>
> And of a palm it dreameth
> That in a Southern land,
> Lonely and silent standeth
> Amid the drifting sand."

There was passion, protest, longing in the music, and the refrain died away and came again like the sobs of a broken heart.

Richard bent over her and looked into her eyes, dark with unshed tears. His voice trembled as he whispered, —

"I am so sorry for you."

She arose and stood before him, a peculiar smile on her face.

"Isn't it hard," she said, "to distinguish between the real and the unreal? When we go together into the unknown land, we seem to have been friends for ages piled on ages. Then we come back to reality, and I sit down here and we talk about the weather. And that of course is much better. It is, you know, bad form — oh, how weary I am of the phrase — for you to tell me that you're sorry for me."

Richard leaned against the piano and looked down at her thoughtfully.

"Yes — and absurd. Why should I be sorry for you? Suppose, for instance — and of course it is not a possibility — that I should tell my cynical friend Fenton, of whom I want to talk to you sometime, that I had met a woman young, beautiful, wealthy, courted by society, wonderfully accomplished, a musician possessing genius, a soul sensitive to all that is noble and beautiful in life, and that I had expressed to her my commiseration. What would he say?"

"Probably," suggested Mrs. Percy-Bartlett, with a note of recklessness in her voice, "your friend Fenton, if he is a man of the world, — and he probably is, as you call him cynical, — would ask you if this unhappy being was married or unmarried. If you told him she was free " —

"Well?"

"Well, he would advise you to check your sympathy and defend your own freedom."

"And if I said that she was married?"

"He would say that you must have known her a long time to take such a liberty." The words were robbed of their harshness by the smile that accompanied them.

"Forgive me, please," he pleaded, bending over her. "How can I help it if words come unbidden to my lips, if I forget that I have known you only a few hours? Won't you absolve me before I go?"

She stood up and gave him her hand.

"I have forgiven you," she said. " It was my fault. You are too sensitive to music."

Then with that charming inconsistency that adds so much to woman's fascination and to the sorrows of the world, she continued : —

"Have you an engagement, Mr. Stoughton, for Friday night ? No ? I should so much like to have you join us in our box at the Metropolitan that evening. 'Sanson et Dalila' is to be given for the first time in this country, you know. Would you care to hear it ? "

" It is very good of you," he said, taking her outstretched hand. "How much pleasure your invitation gives me I dare not tell you — for fear of taking a liberty."

She smiled merrily at his little shaft of sarcasm, and he left her with the roguish light still dancing in her eyes.

She turned and walked across the drawing-room and wandered aimlessly into the library. Soon she found herself seated at the piano, but there was no comfort there. For the first time

within her recollection her bosom friend, her
confidante, the sharer of her joys and sorrows,
had turned false.

Throwing herself down upon a divan, she
buried her head in the pillows and sobbed
bitterly.

CHAPTER V.

"One robbery does not justify another."

So said Richard Stoughton to John Fenton as they sat at dinner in the restaurant of the Astor House, while the wind and the snow played tag up and down Broadway, and men compared the blizzard of '88 with the storm that was then raging, and incidentally wondered how the star-eyed goddess of Reform enjoyed cleaning the streets.

It was Friday evening, and Richard was hurrying his dinner that he might reach his rooms in time to dress for the opera. He and Fenton had just come from a visit to a tenement house not far from the famous hotel in which they were seated, and their conversation had naturally turned upon the great problem suggested by the sights they had witnessed.

"Come with me," Fenton had said to the younger man an hour before. "I want to show you a picture that will make a striking contrast to the scene you will witness at the Metropolitan to-night."

Somewhat against his will, Richard had consented to accompany Fenton, and they had found a family in a garret, starving and freezing, almost within a stone's throw of the City Hall. It had been a painful experience, no less to Fenton, whose long years in active newspaper life had accustomed him to the phenomena that vice and poverty exhibit in a great city, than to the younger man, whose life had been spent in the sunny haunts of prosperity, and who knew little of the outward aspects of human misery beyond what his imagination could picture.

"Explain yourself," said Fenton rather sternly, refilling his sherry glass.

"What I mean is simple enough," answered Richard. "I have read the books you gave me, and I acknowledge they have presented a startling picture of the horrors that result, seemingly, from the unequal distribution of wealth. I think I am even willing to admit that, theoretically, nobody can show any very satisfactory claim to even a square foot of the earth's surface. But it is one thing arguing in the abstract, and another looking at life in the concrete. Granting, for instance, that my ancestors stole land from the Indians, who may have taken it by force from some prehistoric race, is that any reason why those who believe in a new method of taxation should wrest my property from me?"

A smile, both sad and sarcastic, lingered about Fenton's firm, unsymmetrical mouth.

"I have played my game with you and lost, Richard," he said at length, lighting a cigar, while his companion sipped a *demi-tasse* of coffee, "and, on the whole, I am not surprised. Neither am I especially sorry. The economic theories toward which I was trying to direct your steps are not such as lead to peace of mind. Had you become an enthusiast in the great crusade for the introduction of the millennium, you would have grown old before your time, the pressure of things that are would crush you in your effort to hold to the things that should be, and I would have been responsible for making you a discontented and restless being like myself. I told you at the outset that I was not in the habit of trying to make converts to the views of my master. Why I experimented with you I can hardly say. I hope you'll forgive me."

The gentle, affectionate smile on Fenton's face was an unwonted visitor to that stern countenance. Richard impulsively put out his hand to his friend.

"There is nothing to forgive, old man. I realize the unselfishness that prompts you to long for a change in the conditions that beget so much human suffering. Don't think that I am so heartless that the scenes we have just witnessed do not affect me. They do; and I fully understand that the future has the greatest problem of all the ages yet to solve. But you cannot wonder, John Fenton, that at my age and with my prospects it is hard for me to take the whole human race to my heart, and try to remedy wrongs for which I am in no way responsible."

Fenton puffed his cigar in silence for a while. Finally he said, more as if he spoke to himself than to his companion, —

"Yes, youth is *so* strong; but the pleasures of life weave their web, and the hour of strength goes by! To-night youth and wealth and beauty will gather to hear an allegory, — an allegory centuries old, — the ancient, impressive story of Samson and Delilah. In that vast throng will there be one who reads in that old biblical legend the story of the hour? Will they see in Samson the figure of American youth, glorious in its strength, falling a victim to the wiles of the temptress? They will see this same man of power, who has desecrated the precious heritage intrusted to him, blind, maddened by the suffering he has brought upon himself, pulling down in his frenzy the gorgeous structure above his devoted head; and they will go away to their clubs and ball-rooms and supper-parties, and discuss Mantelli's voice, and Tamagno's conception of his *rôle*.

"'Oh, let the strücken deer go weep, the hart ungallëd play,
For some must watch, while some must weep — so runs the
     world away.'

The older I grow, Richard, the more I am amazed at Shakespeare's thorough grasp of human nature as we find it at the end of the nineteenth century."

Richard arose and donned his overcoat.

"Well, John," he remarked smilingly, "I'll compromise with you, then ; I'll read Shakespeare instead of the contemporary writer to whom you have introduced me ; and thus your hope for my redemption may still be kept alive."

Fenton made no answer, and a moment later they stood at the door, looking through the frost-covered glass upon the wind-swept street. For an instant they hesitated to plunge into the wintry blast. Suddenly Fenton turned to his companion.

"How did Mrs. Percy-Bartlett impress you, Richard ?"

The unexpectedness of the question caused the young man to start nervously.

"I find her," he answered hesitatingly, " a very charming woman."

"Yes, I believe you do," returned Fenton gruffly.

Then he pushed open the doors, and made his way hurriedly across Broadway, leaving Richard Stoughton standing on the hotel steps, gazing wonderingly at the retreating figure of his eccentric friend.

CHAPTER VI.

In spite of the storm, a large audience had gathered at the Metropolitan Opera House. The first rendition of Saint-Saëns's opera, "Sanson et Dalila" had been a magnet to the multitude that can endure a biblical story if it is presented to them in an attractive setting. As the irreverent Buchanan Budd had whispered to Mrs. Percy-Bartlett, "The Old Testament is full of unused librettos. But it is strange that the 'first lesson' of this evening's service should come to us from wicked Paris."

The Percy-Bartletts' parterre-box contained four persons as the curtain arose, the stage showing the unhappy Hebrews mourning the desertion of Jehovah, and the afflictions forced upon them by the priests of Dagon, the fish-god.

Just in front of Richard Stoughton sat

Gertrude Van Vleck, for the time being Mrs. Percy-Bartlett's most intimate friend. This means, of course, that they confided in each other in a gingerly way, and spoke of each other in terms of enthusiastic admiration to third persons.

Gertrude Van Vleck had been a reigning belle for two seasons. Society had received her with a good deal of enthusiasm. She was rich, handsome, — in a rather striking style, — and her blood was as blue as any that a new country can produce. But, after her first appearance as a *débutante*, Gertrude Van Vleck had not been especially popular in the inner circle. She had had many suitors of course, but her indifference to their wooing had been the occasion of remark. But this was not all. From her mother, who had come from an old New England family, Gertrude had inherited a strain of Yankee humor that was not appreciated by the set in which she moved. The whisper had been spread abroad in her first season that she had said several really clever things, and a good many

conservative people had considered this an
erratic tendency on her part that was distinctly dangerous. Society did not feel certain that Gertrude Van Vleck might not at
any moment perpetrate a witticism that would
scratch the face of its most cherished traditions. The worst of it was that her position
in society was so firmly established that she
could afford to indulge her appreciation of the
ludicrous and her inclination to look at things
in an original way. Society was powerless to
discipline her.

Furthermore, it was suspected that Gertrude Van Vleck was in sympathy with the
effort of woman to break away from her time-
honored subserviency to man, and to do a
great deal of independent thinking about the
problems that agitate the world. She had
given her countenance to the efforts of women
to turn the political scale at the last election
into the lap of reform, — whatever that elusive
thing may be, — and she had been a pioneer
in the movement that had gained recognition
for the bicycle from the swell set.

Richard Stoughton had heard something of all this; and he found himself looking at Gertrude with considerable curiosity, while the Hebrews were airing their woes upon the stage — woes that awakened little sympathy from an audience that knew how well in latter days the oppressed race has triumphed over all obstacles, and has placed a mortgage on a planet that has practically refused them a native land. Richard admitted to himself that Miss Van Vleck was handsome, that her eyes were of a cerulean tint worthy of her blood, that her dark hair was strikingly effective, that her white neck and arms were well cut. He also felt that nothing too bitter to please a man or woman of sense could fall from a mouth so finely shaped as hers.

Nevertheless, he turned from the contemplation of Gertrude's statuesque beauty to glance at the softer, but equally effective, radiance of Mrs. Percy-Bartlett; and their eyes met for the first time since he had entered the box. Richard felt that the sympathy that had seemed to exist between himself and Mrs. Percy-Bartlett

at their first meeting was not a dream, but a
reality ; that the unrest he had experienced
since he had looked into her brown eyes on
parting with her a few nights before could still
find relief when he gazed into those eyes again.
She smiled, and leaned toward him.

"I am not in the mood for oratorio, as this
first act seems to be," she whispered. "I'd
rather talk to you."

Richard bent nearer to her. The perfume
of her hair thrilled him with a subtle ecstasy.

"I have much to say to you," he answered,
"about — about" —

"About what?" she murmured, smiling at
his hesitancy.

"About yourself. Myself — the last few days
— about a thousand things that — that might
bore you."

"Then don't say them," she remarked. "I
cannot bear to be bored."

She turned to look at the stage, and Richard felt a pang of annoyance at her coquetry.
Had he been a few years older, a bit more
experienced in the ways of woman, he would

have been pleased at her treatment of him. A woman does not waste coquetry on a man in whom she is not interested.

Buchanan Budd and Gertrude Van Vleck were good friends. As there had never been anything warmer in their acquaintanceship than a keen appreciation of each other's mental alertness, they took solid pleasure in each other's society. Budd was a rather clever fellow by nature; but he had never let his cleverness go beyond the bonds of strict propriety. Having attained a much higher place in society than his parents had occupied, he conformed with almost religious reverence to the forms and edicts prescribed by the leaders of the circle in which he occupied a somewhat precarious position. He was a handsome man, and had inherited a large fortune; and so society had overlooked the fact that his immediate ancestors had been in trade, and had admitted him into its sacred precincts. Nevertheless, he had never felt quite assured of his position, and had made it a practice to walk in the very narrow groove paced by the leaders of his set.

"Do you not find food for reflection?" he whispered to Gertrude Van Vleck, during the second act of the opera, "in this unhappy story of woman's interference in public affairs?"

She turned her dark blue eyes on him, and smiled coldly.

"There are women and women," she returned. "It was Samson's weakness that brought disaster to himself and his people."

"I acknowledge my defeat," said Budd humbly. "I have nothing to say for Samson, excepting that he sings rather well."

"That is graceful of you. But, frankly, Mr. Budd, you don't approve of woman going into public life, and riding the bicycle?"

"Whether I do or do not makes little difference, Miss Van Vleck. The time is past when the opinion of men regarding these matters has any weight. The wise man to-day is he who frankly acknowledges that he is no longer a lord of creation, and settles down to suffer in silence, and to adapt himself to the new conditions."

Gertrude's eyes twinkled merrily.

"What a sad picture!" she exclaimed under her breath. "I am as sorry for you as for that poor Hebrew giant, with his shorn locks and his sightless eyes. But I am very glad, Mr. Budd, that you are not inclined to pull down the temple about our heads."

Richard had been talking to Mrs. Percy-Bartlett about John Fenton.

"You interest me in the man," she said earnestly. "I have a vague idea of having heard Mr. Percy-Bartlett speak of him as a brilliant but eccentric man of good origin, who cut quite a figure in society fifteen or twenty years ago. I think he had an unhappy love-affair that drove him into dissipation. Then he squandered his fortune, and dropped out of sight."

"I did not know all this," said Richard musingly; "but it explains several things. At all events, Fenton has exercised a great fascination over me. I really like him better than any man I have met in New York. This is the more peculiar, as I am not in sympathy with any idea or theory that he propounds. It is strange how we are drawn to or repelled by people, without being able to explain just why we like one man and detest another, why one woman makes us misogynistic, and another causes us to forget everying but the heaven that lies in her" —

Richard hesitated.

"Well ? " whispered Mrs. Percy-Bartlett, glancing up at him rather shyly.

"The heaven that lies in her deep, brown eyes," he murmured recklessly, as the house broke into applause after a thrilling duet between Samson and Delilah.

As the opera neared its conclusion, Mrs. Percy-Bartlett, who had been gazing thoughtfully at the stage without seeming to be much impressed by the drama enacted there, turned to Richard, and said, —

"I am to have a small musicale on Tuesday evening. Do you think you could persuade Mr. Fenton to come to it ? "

Richard looked at her a moment in silence. He was surprised at her proposal.

"I cannot answer for him," he said at length. "He is very eccentric."

"That is why I want him to come," returned Mrs. Percy-Bartlett stubbornly. " There is something in his career and in his personality, as you describe it, that leads me to try an experiment with him."

Richard glanced at her questioningly. He did not quite approve of her at that moment. She seemed to understand the expression on his face.

"I want him to meet Gertrude Van Vleck," she explained, smiling at him frankly.

Richard returned her smile, and said, "I will bring him if I can;" then he added after a pause, "but the age of miracles has passed."

CHAPTER VII.

"He certainly has an extremely attractive face, Harriet," remarked Gertrude Van Vleck, looking at Mrs. Percy-Bartlett amusedly; "but isn't he very young?"

"Perhaps he is in one sense," assented the elder woman, striking a few chords on the piano impatiently. "But he's exactly my age —and I'm very old."

Gertrude laughed and settled herself comfortably in an easy-chair for a confidential chat with her bosom friend. It was early in the afternoon of a brilliant winter day, and the music-room of the Percy-Bartletts' house was a very cosey little confessional at the moment.

"I wish I could like men somewhere near my own age," mused Gertrude, her eyes still resting thoughtfully on her companion's rather disturbed face. "But I can't; there really seems to be something fatally wrong in my inclina-

tions and disinclinations.   There is something
authoritative about a man of forty that pleases
me.   But in our set the men at forty are either
married impossibilities or confirmed bachelors."

Mrs. Percy-Bartlett laughed merrily.

" How we do crave contrasts," she exclaimed.
" You are suffering from too much attention
from boys just out of college, and I — well, I'm
married to a man nearly forty."

" After all, Harriet, I don't believe that age
has so much to do with it as we seem to imply."   Gertrude clasped her hands around her
knee as she sat leaning forward, and looked
up at her friend earnestly.   " There is one
thing that the new movement among the women
of our class has done.   It has tended to weary
us of men who are all cut on one pattern.
Take any given subject of any importance and
ask one of the men of our set what he thinks
about it.   Dear little parrot, he will repeat to
you the general verdict of his club on the
question at issue, without the slightest suspicion that he is a mental marionette."

" That is very true," assented Mrs. Percy-

Bartlett. "Perhaps that fact may explain to you why I enjoy talking to Richard Stoughton."

"Oh," cried Gertrude, her face displaying an animation that it seldom exhibited in public. "Then he is not yet spoiled by the churning process? He certainly carries himself like other society men of his age. His face is brighter than the average youngster's, but another season will change all that."

Mrs. Percy-Bartlett swung around on the music-stool and looked earnestly into Gertrude's face.

"He's not a society man, my dear girl. He *could* have the *entrée* if he wanted it. His people are very prominent in Connecticut, and he was in the best set at Yale. But, do you know, although he has plenty of money, he is quite ambitious in a very queer line."

"Yes?" questioned Gertrude, curious regarding her friend's feelings toward Richard.

"Yes. He is a newspaper man. He's on the *Trumpet*, you know, and has been wonderfully successful in some way or other. He writes awfully bright things for the editorial page. Percy-Bartlett says that it is a most unusual thing for a man as young as Richard Stoughton to jump at a bound into such a prominent position."

"A newspaper man. Isn't that amusing! I never met one before."

"Well," commented the musician, turning around and drumming softly on the piano, "there is one thing to be said about them; they have to be bright, or they couldn't be newspaper men."

"That is a very sweeping assertion," remarked Gertrude, smiling in amusement. "I wonder if it applies to newspaper women."

"I don't know; I never met one," answered Mrs. Percy-Bartlett coldly.

"But tell me," persisted Gertrude, her blue eyes dark with mischief; "what are you going to do with him?"

Almost unconsciously Mrs. Percy-Bartlett began to play the air she had composed to Heine's poem on the pine-tree that dreamed of the palm. Suddenly she ceased playing, and gazed earnestly at Gertrude.

"I don't know," she said at length, and the roguish light died out of Gertrude's eyes.

"I don't understand you, Harriet," she said very seriously. "You don't mean that — that " —

"I mean nothing," cried Mrs. Percy-Bartlett rather feverishly, turning to the piano and playing a few bars of the latest waltz music. Presently she turned around and said, —

"You are unkind, Gertrude. You are unmarried, unengaged, and you can take as much interest as you may care to in any man, married or otherwise, and the world doesn't stop to gossip about you — that is, of course, if you don't go on in a scandalous way. But let a married woman show the slightest attention to a man who is not her husband, and everybody begins to whisper and nod and smile, and you are lucky if *Town Tattle* doesn't begin to hint at another divorce in the inner circle. I don't care how many people sing my songs and admire my music, but I wish they *would* stop talking about *me*. Can you tell me, Gertrude, why I shouldn't have the privilege of talking to

—to Richard Stoughton, for instance, without being gossiped about?"

"The trouble is, you know, Harriet," answered Gertrude, the mischievous gleam returning to her eye, "that whatever may be the case with marriage, it was long ago decided that Platonic friendship is a failure."

"Perhaps so," returned Mrs. Percy-Bartlett rather wearily. "But people will follow it, *ignis fatuus* though it may be, to the end of time."

Gertrude arose to go. "Well, Harriet," she said softly, bending over and kissing her friend on the forehead, "don't be annoyed at anything I've said. I certainly have the warmest sympathy with your disinclination to let life bore you."

Mrs. Percy-Bartlett arose and took Gertrude's hand. "And you will come to my musicale on Tuesday night, my dear?"

"Indeed I shall. I want to get better acquainted with Mr. Richard Stoughton, you know."

At that moment a servant entered the room and handed a note to her mistress.

"Excuse me, Gertrude," she said, and opening the envelope read the following words from Richard : —

" MY DEAR MRS. PERCY-BARTLETT, — The miracle has been performed. Mr. John Fenton will accompany me to your musicale on Tuesday evening. Your invitation will reach him if addressed to the Press Club."

The reader smiled, and handed the epistle to Gertrude Van Vleck.

"And who is John Fenton?" asked Gertrude, after perusing the note.

"Oh, John Fenton," said Mrs. Percy-Bartlett gayly, "John Fenton is an experiment."

CHAPTER VIII.

"MEETING strangers at a musicale is not always a pleasant experience. If you are musical, the people bore you; if you are sociable, the music bores you."

So John Fenton had said to Richard Stoughton, when the latter had made his first effort to perform a miracle and obtain the former's acceptance in advance of Mrs. Percy-Bartlett's invitation.

"But you owe me this reparation, Fenton," Richard had urged. "When you gave me those books on the single-tax theory to read, did I hold off and say that if I was indifferent the books would bore me, or, if I became a convert, I would bore my friends? No; I made no excuses, but read the books. Now I claim my reward. You have failed, after a fair trial, to make me an advocate of the immediate establishment of the millennium. Let me

now have an equal chance of persuading you
that the best thing to do is to take the world
as we find it, and enjoy the good the gods
provide."

The two men were spending the hour
after dinner in Fenton's bachelor-apartments.
They had fallen into the way of dining
together whenever they were both free to do
so; and their friendship, having withstood the
failure of Fenton's effort to make the young
man an economic radical, had grown warmer
as the weeks went by. In several ways Fenton
had derived considerable benefit from his close
intercourse with Stoughton. It had been
remarked in the city room of the *Trumpet* that
Fenton had given up drinking cocktails, and
that he had grown particular about his attire.
He no longer allowed his hair and beard to
show signs of neglect; and the reporters for
the paper had said to each other that the
assistant editor did not seem to be quite as
sarcastic and testy as he had been in former
times. But if any one had told Fenton that
a youth not long out of college, and of a mental

make-up that was dazzling rather than con-
vincing, had been the active cause in begetting
certain reforms in his habits of life, the cynical
and time-scarred journalist would have considered his informant insane. The strongest men
are moulded and remoulded by their friends,
but they are seldom willing to acknowledge
the fact.

After Richard's last argument, Fenton had
puffed his cigar in silence for a time. But he
was not thinking of what his companion had
just said. He had grown convinced from several remarks, dropped inadvertently by his
friend, that the young man had become very
much interested in Mrs. Percy-Bartlett. It
was not within the possibilities of their exist-
ing friendship for him to question Richard very
closely on this point; but he was extremely
anxious to know the exact truth of the matter.
If he went to the musicale, he thought, he
could see for himself just how the affair stood,
and would be the better able to guide his own
steps in the premises. It had been his passion, when a young man, for a certain married

woman, that had ruined John Fenton. He had a well-grounded horror, therefore, of seeing Richard Stoughton wrecking himself on the same rock that had caused his own downfall.

"You have stated your arguments very cleverly, Richard," he had said, after a time. "You sacrificed yourself on the altar of my books. I will reciprocate by throwing myself under the juggernaut of your musicale. But, understand me, you will be disappointed in the result. Society has no allurements for me. I touched it at all points years ago, when I had much more enthusiasm than I have now ; and, I tell you, there is nothing in it as a permanent amusement for a man of sense. What is a gathering of people of fashion, at its best ? Nothing more than a dress-parade of more or less well-groomed men and women who revenge themselves for boring each other in public by destroying each other's characters in private."

"If you ever have time," suggested Richard, smiling, "you should write a novel, John. You have a way of scolding the universe with a kind of epigrammatic fervor that might prove popular."

"You flatter me, Richard, by the implied conviction that I have not yet been flippant enough to produce a work of fiction. I don't want you to idealize me; so I might as well confess, that, years ago, when I was about your age, I did write a novel." Fenton looked at Richard with an expression on his face that would have fitted the confession of a crime. Then he stepped to a closet, and, after rummaging around for a while, brought forth a dust-covered roll of manuscript.

"This," he said, "is one of the little grave-stones in my very large cemetery of dead hopes and dreams."

He brushed the dust off of the roll with almost reverent hand.

"I haven't looked at this thing for years, Richard. I'd almost forgotten about it, until you made that remark about my writing a novel. I have a sort of indistinct idea that, in the storehouse of your ambitions, you have high literary aspirations, more or less concealed from view. If you have, let this, my boy, be a warning to you not to waste your time on a novel."

Richard had been looking through the manuscript with an unaffected show of interest.

"You call it 'Ephemeræ,'" he remarked. "It is a taking title."

"But it didn't take the publishers," returned Fenton, whose face had grown unusually animated by the unexpected revival of long-buried emotions. He had put a good deal of the energy, enthusiasm, and vigor of early manhood into the rejected novel, and it had received the minute polish that his life of leisure at that time had enabled him to give it. How bitterly disappointed he had been at its refusal by a leading publishing house he had long forgotten; but the present moment had brought back to him a multitude of conflicting emotions, changed by time into a general feeling of regret and self-pity.

"My writing is rather blind," he remarked, taking the manuscript from his friend. "Let me read you the prologue; not for publication, but as an evidence of good faith."

For the first time in their acquaintanceship, Fenton's unsymmetrical face appeared actually handsome in Richard's eyes. The spirit of the past that lurks in the relics of by-gone years had gently spoken from the dust-stained manuscript, and had bidden John Fenton's lost youth to gleam again in his eyes, and to add a note of enthusiasm to his voice.

" It was a strangely pessimistic piece of work for a man as young as I was at that time to write," he said musingly. "But, as I can say now, after years have strengthened my judgment, this novel is strong and artistic. At the time when it was sent to the publishers, there was little chance for the acceptance of anything written by an American that was not strictly moral and what the good old fossils of that day were so fond of calling 'wholesome.' This is the prologue, Richard. It gives the keynote to the story."

Fenton leaned back in his chair, and read aloud the opening words of his novel : —

" It was not a pretty fly, but it loved the sun. It rejoiced in the power of its wings, the length of its antennæ, the pulsing health of its little body. It was summer, and the fly flitted about in the warm and caressing atmosphere, as though God smiled for its especial pleasure.

"Oh, the glory of the day! No shadow saw the fly, for it soared so high that nought but the golden glory of a smiling universe met its gaze.

"But when the day was done, the little fly was dead.

"It never knew, the joyous trifler, that it was only one of a group of neuropterous insects, belonging to the genus Ephemera, that live in the adult or winged state for a single day, and die when the darkness falls."

There was silence for a moment. Then Richard said : —

"I feel sure, John, that if I had picked up a novel containing that prologue my curiosity would have been piqued; that I would have been anxious to read on to see how the author had made his story harmonize with his melancholy text."

"I remember," said Fenton, lighting a fresh

cigar, and rambling on musingly, "that when I conceived the story I was actuated by the feeling that men take themselves and their affairs too seriously. There seemed to me to be something grimly ludicrous about the vast majority of men, who fuss around for a few years on an insignificant planet in an out-of-the-way corner of space, as if they had been placed here for eternity, and were individually of tremendous significance to the universe at large. I worked out the story on lines intended to show, in a comparatively small compass, that we are as powerless and unimportant in the infinite realm of existence as the foolish little flies that buzz so loud on a summer's day. If I should re-write the story to-day, I am not quite sure that I should take so hopeless a view of the significance of human life. As I have grown older, I have become more inclined to think that no man has a right to consider himself of no importance in the *tout ensemble* of the universe; not, at least, until it is proved conclusively that there is no such thing as a soul possessing eternal life.

At all events, if we are *ephemeræ*, I am sure
that one fly has as much right as another to
the sunshine of the noonday. And so I make
of an economic theory a religion, — for want
of a better." Fenton's sarcastic smile played
across his mouth again as he ceased speaking.

Richard had put on his overcoat, and was
holding out his hand for the manuscript of
Fenton's novel.

"Let me take the story with me, John,"
he said. "I want to read it. I am rather
inclined to think, from what I know of the
present literary market, that now is the appointed time for you to win fame in the realm
of letters."

Fenton, after a moment's hesitancy, handed
the scroll to his friend.

"I am not ambitious in that line," he said
firmly; "but it will do no harm to have you
read the book."

"And you will go to Mrs. Percy-Bartlett's
with me?" Richard exclaimed smilingly. "I
am very glad, John, I assure you. I'm sure

that our hostess will feel that you have paid her a great compliment."

Fenton smiled, almost bitterly; and, as if memory had sharpened his tongue, he said, as he held Richard's hand a moment, —

"I gave that up long ago, my boy. Paying a compliment to a woman is like giving sugar-plums to a child. It establishes a precedent, and begets an appetite. Never tell a woman a thing you don't mean, Richard; especially a married woman."

CHAPTER IX.

"Men used to be divided into two classes, you know, Mr. Fenton, — those who belonged to our set, and those who did not."

Gertrude Van Vleck and John Fenton had retired to a remote corner of Mrs. Percy-Bartlett's drawing-room, and were keeping up as animated a conversation as the depressing influences of a musicale permit. In evening dress, Fenton was a man of a most impressive presence. He had come to Mrs. Percy-Bartlett's musicale expecting to be bored. The expression on his strong, thoughtful face, as he gazed smilingly at the handsome, aristocratic-looking girl beside him, proved that she had followed in Richard Stoughton's footsteps, and had performed a miracle.

"And what is the distinction that you yourself make, Miss Van Vleck?" asked Fenton.

She looked at him earnestly a moment.

"To me," she answered, "there are two kinds of men, — those who interest me, and those who do not."

"Perhaps," said Fenton, taking advantage of an interlude in the music-room, "perhaps it is inconsiderate on my part to ask the question, but I acknowledge that I am curious to know what ratio exists between the men who interest you and the men who do not."

"I don't know that I ever put the problem on a mathematical basis," answered Gertrude, an amused smile playing across her face. "I am inclined to think that the ratio changes from year to year."

"To your advantage?" he asked.

"I'm afraid not. As time goes on I find that I meet more men who do not interest me and fewer who do. But there is compensation for this in the fact that women have grown more attractive to each other than they used to be."

An enthusiastic soprano was at the moment striking certain high notes as though she had a grudge against them, and Fenton was obliged to pause a moment before he asked, —

"Won't you explain that to me, Miss Van
Vleck? It is, as you put it, a novel idea."

"Why, don't you see," she said earnestly,
"the very fact that women are joined together
in a protest against ancient customs and prejudices has drawn them closer to each other;
while, at the same time, it has tended to bring
out the most characteristic qualities of each individual woman. In a word, we women interest each other more as rebels than we did as
slaves."

Again the soprano uttered her protest against
peace and quiet, and Fenton had an opportunity
to weigh Gertrude Van Vleck's words. His
vis-à-vis was a social product the like of which
had not existed in the days when he had been
a member of New York's inner circle, and had
expected from a young unmarried woman nothing in a conversational way that would chal-
lenge thought. Of course, in his journalistic
occupation he had been obliged to follow in
detail the progress of woman toward a broader,
perhaps higher, plane of endeavor; but this was
the first time that Fenton had come face to

face with the new ideas incarnate. He was
entertained, stimulated, inspired, by the experience. At first he had looked upon Gertrude
Van Vleck simply as a finely developed speci-
men of the patrician type, whose dark hair,
deep blue eyes, and finely rounded neck formed
a combination very pleasing to the eye, and
indicated a remote Spanish strain mingling
with her Dutch blood. But after a few moments in her companionship, he had discovered
that she not only satisfied his æsthetic nature,
but piqued his intellectual make-up. She had
given him the highest pleasure that one mind
can bestow upon another, by opening up new
vistas of thought to him.

John Fenton had reached that period of a
life that had been filled with disappointments
when feminine sympathy and appreciation are
among the few things left in the world that
are wholly satisfying. Perhaps it was this very
fact that had led him to make a friend of
Richard Stoughton, a youth whose quick intui-
tions and mental alertness had much in them
that was feminine.

There was, furthermore, a note of defiance in Gertrude's last remark that struck a sympathetic chord in Fenton's nature. No man can accept the premises upon which the economic theories to which Fenton had subscribed are based without developing the rebellious tendencies that lie more or less dormant in all men. For the first time, the similarity impressed him that exists between woman's revolt against the oppression of man, and man's restlessness under the threatening inequalities of wealth.

"And as rebels women are much more attractive to men than they were as conformists," remarked Fenton, seizing an opportunity to resume the conversation, after a self-satisfied tenor had proved to his own satisfaction that he had a divine right to be conceited about his voice. "To use a rather shop-worn quotation, 'Blessings brighten as they take their flight.'"

"But that is not a fair illustration," exclaimed Gertrude earnestly. "We are not trying to fly away from men, but to fly with them."

"That may be true," said Fenton, smiling thoughtfully; "but men are naturally startled at the suddenly displayed power of your wings, and are a little shy at first."

"Why should they be? After all, I believe that the underlying ambition of the new woman — as she is rather vulgarly called — is to make herself intellectually attractive to the brightest men."

"Then the progress of woman has not decreased the social importance of the clever man?" asked Fenton humbly.

"On the contrary, Mr. Fenton, it has enhanced it — by giving him a larger and more appreciative audience. The man of mental power would hold a higher place in a community containing many Mesdames de Staël than in a social circle possessing only one. Is it not so?"

"Do you know, Miss Van Vleck," said Fenton, not answering her question directly, "that I begin to think that I shall owe you a great debt of gratitude?"

A slight tinge of red mounted to her face as

her eyes met his. He impressed her as a man more fitted to bestow favors than to accept them.

"I don't quite understand you," she said softly.

"We owe much," he continued, "to those who take us out of our mental grooves and give us a new standpoint from which to view the world. There may be a good deal of selfishness in occupying one's mind entirely with man's inhumanity to man, and blinding ourselves to man's inhumanity to woman. I have to thank you for a new point of view."

"But," protested Gertrude, "I have said nothing that we do not read in print every day."

"Even if that is so," said Fenton, "truths that would make no impression on me if I read them on an editorial page come to me with startling force when you present them. I repeat, that I owe you a debt of gratitude."

At that moment Mrs. Percy-Bartlett's voice, a rich, highly-cultivated contralto, was heard, giving passionate expression to Heine's mournful little story of the pine that dreamt of love. Richard Stoughton stood at the entrance to the music-room, forgetful of the crowd around him. There was something in her voice that seemed to be meant for him alone, something that told him she was thinking of the night when she had first sung the song to him. "I must be growing wofully egotistic," he thought; but at that instant their eyes met, and his self-depreciation vanished.

She came to him after the applause had died away, and called his attention to an unoccupied corner of the drawing-room.

"I want to talk to you," she said simply. "Come!"

"Do you know," she began playfully, after they were seated, "I have begun to feel a good deal awed in your presence. A man who can perform miracles, you know" —

"Well?" exclaimed Richard, as she hesitated a moment.

"A man who can perform miracles is to be avoided. Just think of poor Trilby and Svengali."

Richard laughed outright.

"That is a most complimentary remark! If I follow you, you mean that I hypnotized John Fenton. I certainly feel flattered. But, do you know, I begin to suspect that your friend, Miss Van Vleck, will prove a much more successful medium than I?"

They both glanced at Gertrude and John Fenton, who were deep in conversation in the opposite corner of the drawing-room.

"I am very glad that all responsibility for the man's future has been taken off of my hands," said Richard. "The fact is, I feel that I have all that I can do to take care of myself."

He looked into her eyes with an expression in his own that was hardly allowable — even at a musicale.

"How selfish a man is," Mrs. Percy-Bartlett murmured musingly. "It is almost impossible for him to be a consistent friend to another man. How much less is he able to be a true friend to a woman."

"The basis of all friendship is affection,"

argued Richard, lowering his voice as the music of a 'cello crept softly through the room. "And affection is a very hard thing to hold in check."

She looked up at him with a smile on her lips, but an expression of sadness in her eloquent brown eyes.

"It is, indeed!" she almost whispered. Then, as if regretting the admission, she leaned back in her chair, and seemed to listen to the soft, throbbing harmonies that the piano and the 'cello begot as their tones met and mingled, as though they caressed each other.

Richard bent forward, and their eyes met again.

"Do you reject my — my friendship?" he whispered.

Suddenly he felt her hand in his; and she smiled as he pressed it, while her eyes brightened, and her cheeks flushed. Withdrawing her hand, she said, her voice hardly audible even as he bent his face close to hers: —

"Remember that there is another foundation-stone to friendship: it is unselfishness."

The words, and the pleading tone in which they were uttered, combined to make her remark sound more like a prayer to his generosity than a statement founded on a time-worn truth.

"I will try," whispered Richard earnestly, "I will try to be an ideal friend to you. I would rather have your friendship than the love of any other woman in the world."

She smiled up at him gratefully, as though he had made a great sacrifice for her happiness. They say that Love is blind. Perhaps that is the reason that the little rascal is such a consummate liar. How can one expect a sightless imp, whose domain is youth, and whose throne is the heart, to wield his sceptre with absolute respectability? If he could see further, Cupid might behave better as a monarch; but the chances are, in that case, that he would be compelled to abdicate.

The hour was waxing late.

"I must resume my duties," said Mrs. Percy-Bartlett reluctantly; "and abandon my friend for the sake of my guests. Will you come

to see me soon? Let me see — a week from
to-night I have no engagement. Will you
come and talk to me of friendship?"

"Very gladly," murmured Richard, touching
her willing hand again. "Until then I shall
not live, but dream!"

Richard and Fenton strolled together down
the avenue, silent and self-absorbed. Finally
the former asked, —

"Did you have a pleasant evening, John?"

"Very," answered Fenton gruffly.

They walked for half a block before they
spoke again.

"The music was well done," ventured Richard.

"Yes," assented Fenton. Neither of the
two again opened their lips until they reached
the cross-street at which they were to part.

"Good-night, John," said Richard, holding
out his hand.

"Good-night, boy! See you to-morrow,"
exclaimed Fenton hurriedly. Then he walked
onward alone.

"I went there," he was saying to himself,
"to get a line on the youngster's affair. But

the cold, hard fact is that I forgot all about him." . . .

At that same moment Percy-Bartlett and Buchanan Budd were smoking their good-night cigars together at the club.

"It is really too bad," Budd was saying, "that the newspapers have been able to print so much scandal about our set. But I suppose there is no way to prevent it."

"But there is a way," returned Percy-Bartlett almost sternly. "What we need in the inner circle is more heroism and less heroics. If *noblesse oblige* means anything at all in these days, it demands of those who live up to its behests that they be self-contained, not hysterical. There is no necessity for a domestic tragedy getting into print if the man or woman who is wronged is fundamentally worthy of a place in the most select coterie on earth."

"You would rather wink at crime than have the public gossip about you, then?" asked Budd.

"I would — a thousand times!" answered Percy-Bartlett, throwing away his cigar and saying "good-night" cheerily.

CHAPTER X.

"I AM not in the mood for listening to the confessions of a frivolous boy," remarked John Fenton, looking up from his desk in the city room of the *Trumpet* at Richard Stoughton on the afternoon following Mrs. Percy-Bartlett's musicale.

"Don't be cross with me, John," implored Richard gently; "I have no intention of worrying you with my peccadilloes. But I want you to look in on me for an hour after dinner. I really have a very important matter I want to talk to you about. You aren't on duty to-night, are you?"

"No," answered Fenton, with apparent reluctance. Then he hesitated a moment, and finally said, —

"Very well, Richard. I'll do you the great honor of calling on you about half after seven. But I give you fair warning, if you begin to bore me, I shall fly at once."

"It's a bargain!" exclaimed the youth, as he turned away.

Richard occupied a rather luxurious suite of bachelor-apartments on a side-street not very far up-town. As he sat before an open fire after dinner that evening awaiting the arrival of John Fenton, he felt thoroughly contented with himself and the world at large. He had come to New York unknown and unheralded, and lo! the great city, so indifferent to the advent of most strangers, had opened its arms to him, had patted him on the back, had told him that he was clever, and therefore welcome. The great metropolis has an insatiable hunger for able men in all lines of life, but it is often blind for many years to the merits of certain citizens who need only an opportunity to become prominent. Once in a great while, however, it seizes a very young man by the collar of his coat, as it were, and thrusts him forward in some field of endeavor, and the multitude of older men who have failed to take advantage of their life-tide at its flood, look on with mingled amazement and envy at the lucky youth.

Chance had thrown Richard Stoughton into the front ranks of journalism; and as he watched the flickering blaze before him, or followed the smoke from his cigar with his eye, he felt that he was worthy of the position he held, and that the metropolis had not made a blunder when it had picked him out as one entitled to applause.

The door behind Richard opened softly, and John Fenton entered the room and quietly seated himself at the other side of the fireplace.

"Have a cigar, John," said the youth, deserting his air-castles for the stern realities that Fenton always seemed to carry with him. Turning to offer his guest a light, Richard was surprised to see that Fenton was garbed in evening dress. "My miracle is taking on a chronic form," he said to himself. Then aloud he remarked, —

"I thank you, John, for not disappointing me. I have several weighty problems on my mind, and you're the only man of my acquaintance who can help me out."

Fenton puffed away silently for a few moments.

"Go on," he said at length, rather coldly. "You want to talk to me about — what?"

"About the single-tax theory, John, as applied to affairs of the heart."

Fenton glanced sternly at his companion, but there was no sign of mischief on Richard's face. He was gazing at the fire as though trying to read in the dancing flames the answer to the riddle that annoyed him.

"Explain yourself," said Fenton suspiciously.

"Well," went on Richard with studied calmness, "you see, I am trying to get into touch with all the new ideas that have a marked influence on the life of our times. I am, however, especially interested in watching the effect of theories on the actions of my friends. It's almost a new science, I think. I must look up some Greek roots and give it a name. Perhaps I'll go down to fame as the inventor of a new and very useful line of study."

"What are you attempting to get at, Richard?" exclaimed Fenton, twisting around uneasily in his chair and trying to obtain a clear view of the young man's face.

"That's not the point, John. The question is, what are *you* striving to accomplish? You see, I have been doing a good deal of unconscious cerebration in regard to your single-tax ideas, and I have reached a point where I should like to ask a few more questions regarding the demands that your belief makes on your habits of life. . Now, you know, our good old Puritan ancestors were fond of looking upon this world as 'a vale of tears.' You single-tax people go a step farther, and call it 'a den of thieves.'"

"Come, Richard," said Fenton firmly, "don't be flippant."

"The very last thing that I feel inclined to be, John. I'm in sober earnest. Let me ask you a question. You consider, of course, a man who collects rents from property he holds in this city from his ancestors a receiver of stolen goods?"

"Well, what if I do?" asked Fenton testily.

"I was curious to know, that's all."

"And what if I say that I do?" persisted Fenton at length, in a more amenable tone of voice.

"Well, if you do, would you make a bosom friend of a son of this receiver of stolen goods, who will, in all likelihood, come into the booty after a time, and whose blood is tainted by his descent from a line of land-pirates?"

"Nonsense, Richard! I don't see the use of putting those questions to me — just at this time. If a man is by heredity a drunkard I may feel sorry for him, but it is not my duty to express my disapproval of his ancestors so long as he treats me decently."

"That's logical enough," commented Richard enthusiastically. "I really begin to think, John, that you still have sense enough left not to let your economic theories and beliefs — convictions that, I have heard, sometimes make fanatics of those who hold them — ruin any chance that might come to you for great happiness in life."

There was silence in the room for several minutes.

"It's curious," remarked Fenton musingly, "that you have taken just this tack, Richard. You have that faculty of intuition that is, for the most part, a feminine characteristic. I can see evidences of that peculiarity of mind in your work on the editorial page. You seem to reach at a bound deductions that most men would have to work out with painful effort."

"You mean by that, John, that, to use the words of our professional President, it is a condition, not a theory, that confronts you, and that I know it."

"I admit nothing, Richard," said Fenton stubbornly, and looking at his watch.

"But," persisted Richard, as his friend rose to go, "you believe that a man who holds real estate in New York—derived, let us say, from his Dutch ancestors—is the dishonest holder of ill-gotten gain?"

"This is unkind, Richard," said Fenton, with more emotion in his voice than his friend had ever heard it express. "I have neither the inclination nor the time at present to explain my present position."

"Why not the time, John?" asked Richard, smiling mischievously.

"Because, my boy," and Fenton spoke like a man driven to the wall, "I'm going up-town to call on Miss Van Vleck."

Richard laughed outright.

"No wonder," he cried, "that you can't explain your present position."

Richard found himself alone in the room, and, lighting a fresh cigar, reseated himself before the fire.

"It was heroic treatment," he mused, "but it's the only course to pursue with such a man as John Fenton."

Then he fell to thinking of Mrs. Percy-Bartlett, and the hours flew by.

CHAPTER XI.

BUCHANAN BUDD had been doing a good deal of deep thinking of late — proof positive that the times were out of joint. Budd, of course, was obliged to do more or less thinking in order to be always correctly dressed, but it was only a great crisis that could compel him to ponder really weighty problems for any length of time.

When a subterranean disturbance shakes a city it is the most clumsily constructed houses that go down first. In like manner, when the most select circle of society is in trouble, it is the man who has no very good claim to recognition in that circle who first feels the effects of the internal agitation.

As Buchanan Budd listened to the current gossip at his clubs, and read in the newspapers impudent criticisms on the doings of the people with whom he associated, he came reluctantly, but firmly, to the conclusion that it behooved him to take some step that would strengthen his position as a recognized member of the most exclusive social clique in the country — perhaps in the world.

It did not take him long to decide that the only fitting strategical move on his part lay along the line of matrimony. Not that he came to this conviction willingly. He enjoyed life as a bachelor, and he felt that in taking to himself a wife he would be making a most dangerous experiment. He could not blind himself to the fact that the unpleasant publicity at that time being thrust upon certain members of the inner circle had had its origin in unfortunate marriages. Nevertheless, he realized that society expected of him, at some time or other, a personal sacrifice of his liberty on the altar of matrimony; and the present crisis seemed to be an appropriate moment for propitiating the powers controlling the inner circle by taking to himself a wife who would render him safe for the future in any sifting process in which society might indulge.

After going over the list of eligible young women in his set, he had decided, without much hesitation, that Gertrude Van Vleck was, as he put it to himself, the card for him to play. She possessed several characteristics that rendered her especially eligible. In the first place, her position in society was thoroughly assured. Furthermore, she possessed sufficient mental alertness to render her companionable to a man who had not been quite able to crush all fondness for originality out of his make-up. Then again — and this was an important consideration — he had never made love to her. They had been good friends, to use a rather meaningless phrase, and Budd was encouraged by the thought that he had never prejudiced his chances with her by invoking sentiment to add spice to their intercourse.

That she had rejected several suitors was a fact well known to society, and there had been a good deal of discussion as to Gertrude Van Vleck's motive for refusing at least two offers that were generally considered especially desirable. In weighing this phase of the case, Buchanan Budd, who was not an abnormally modest man, asked himself if the explanation of her reluctance to enter into wedlock had not been due to the fact that he, in certain respects one of the most eligible bachelors in the city, had hitherto approached her only as a friend. It is true that she had sometimes appeared to indulge in a little sarcasm at his expense, but her tongue might have been inspired by pique. What more likely than that his failure to put any special warmth into his manner, when she had hoped for something more than friendship, had been the underlying cause of those shafts of satire that she had sometimes launched at him? The more Buchanan Budd questioned himself on this point, the more he became convinced that Gertrude Van Vleck concealed a fondness for him that she only awaited a change in his manner to reveal.

There was one peculiarity possessed by Budd that might have enabled him to earn his own living, if fate had not ordained that he should lie on a bed of roses. When he had decided upon a course of action, he never hesitated to begin operations at once. But, as he seldom reached any conclusion that demanded the exercise of energy and directness, there was something novel and inspiring in the emotions that animated him as he sent in his card to Gertrude Van Vleck on the very evening on which he had pursued, while smoking a cigar at his favorite club, the mental processes outlined above. He felt that there was something Napoleonic in thus moving on the enemy's stronghold at once, and he entered her drawing-room with almost the air of a conqueror. One fact that rendered bachelorhood so satisfactory to Buchanan Budd was that he possessed quite a vivid imagination. No man will grow too lonely if he can constantly delude himself with flattering fancies, and picture himself as the centre of the universe, with the ends of space to do his bidding.

"And what am I to have from you this evening, Mr. Budd?" asked Gertrude, seating

herself for a chat that she knew would prove
amusing. "Censure for the new woman?"

"No, Miss Van Vleck; I crave advice for the
old-fashioned man."

Gertrude smiled, and her eyes flashed merrily as she exclaimed, —

"There is a mystery here! Mr. Buchanan
Budd seeking advice from a woman whom he
suspects of holding advanced ideas! That
seems hardly reasonable."

There was something in Gertrude Van Vleck's
manner and appearance that struck Budd as
unusual. He had always considered her a
handsome woman, but to-night her eyes were
more brilliant, her complexion more dazzling,
than he had ever seen them, while there was
something in the tone of her voice and the
movements of her hands that seemed to indicate suppressed excitement. These phenomena, he argued, augured well for the advance
movement that he, with Napoleonic cleverness,
had determined to order along the entire line
of his attack. But the moment for his forward
movement had not quite come. A little skir-

mishing in the open field was essential before he ordered up his heavy troops.

"But why is it not reasonable, Miss Van Vleck? Surely, even a conservative, and, if you please, reactionary, man may feel anxious to put himself in touch with the new ideas. It may even be that he honestly desires to embrace as many of the iconoclastic theories of the day as possible, if for no other purpose than to retain the friendships he made in the peaceful days before — before " —

"Before the women of our set began to think, you mean," said Gertrude, as he hesitated a moment. "It is certainly complimentary on your part — and so self-sacrificing." There was a touch of sarcasm in her voice.

Budd looked at her appealingly. "You hardly do justice to my motives, Miss Van Vleck. I am honestly anxious to overcome my ancient prejudices and to put myself in sympathy with the age in which I live. You can do *so* much to help me in this — if you will."

There was a note of tenderness in his voice that Gertrude had never heard in it before, and

she glanced at him suspiciously. She had
derived considerable pleasure, in a mild way,
from her friendly intercourse with Buchanan
Budd; and her liking for him had been based,
to a great extent, on the utter absence of flirta-
tiousness in his manner. That he had any
intention of jeopardizing their friendship by
injecting sentiment into the relationship was a
new thought to her. At that moment it was
the most unwelcome suspicion that could have
entered her mind. There is no time when a
woman so dreads the advances of a man to
whom she is indifferent as the moment when
she admits to herself that her heart is influenced by another. Buchanan Budd had unconsciously forced Gertrude Van Vleck into a
self-confession that made her pulse flutter and
her cheek turn pale.

"I fear, Mr. Budd," she went on with nervous vivacity, "that you would not be willing
to follow us very far—no matter how great an
effort I made to put you in sympathy with the
new movement. Let me tell you, Mr. Budd,
there is no predicting where it will all end. A

woman in Vienna has applied to the authorities to be appointed chief-executioner.   A Miss Edith Walker is an applicant in Bogota, Columbia, for the office of chief of police.   I see by your face that you are shocked at all this.   I am so glad."

"Glad that I am shocked?" exclaimed Budd confusedly.

"No, not that; but that I have had the courage to warn you."

"To warn me?"

"Yes," answered Gertrude, the former paleness of her cheeks giving place to a slight flush, "to warn you.   Don't you see that there is great danger in attempting to keep up with the restless activity of the *fin-de-siècle* woman? I think you will be much happier, Mr. Budd, in sticking to your former convictions, and not attempting to take an interest in movements and tendencies with which, you know, you are not in sympathy at heart."

"But," persisted Budd, who felt that somehow his plan of campaign was not working itself out with the success that should attend a truly Napoleonic manœuvre, "I came here to ask you to help me, not by throwing cold water on my aspirations, but by telling me how to become worthy of — of the new woman."

Gertrude Van Vleck laughed nervously.

"I appreciate the compliment you have paid me, Mr. Budd, but I am unworthy of the trust you seem to place in me. Frankly, I find it so difficult to adjust my former, I might say my hereditary, convictions to the teachings of the day, that I feel that I must remain a follower instead of a leader, even at the expense of not winning for the cause so valuable a champion as Mr. Buchanan Budd."

For the first time since he had opened fire, Buchanan Budd realized that his skirmish-line had been driven back. But a battle is never lost until the last charge is made.

"I am sorry," he said in a musing tone, "that you have not given me more encouragement in my effort to — to revise my ideas regarding — regarding woman's sphere, I think you call it. I assure you, Miss Van Vleck," and he bent toward her, "that my motive in asking you to help me in this matter was not of small importance to myself.   I am very anxious to — to " —

He paused for words with a hesitation that was not at all Napoleonic. At that moment a servant entered with a card for Miss Van Vleck.

" Mr. John Fenton ! " exclaimed Gertrude, with something in her voice that did not please Buchanan Budd.

Then she turned calmly toward him and asked, " Do you know Mr. Fenton, Mr. Budd ? "

A hitherto unpublished anecdote tells how a daring onlooker approached Napoleon on the morning of Waterloo and said, —

" Pardon me, Sire, but have you ever met Wellington before ? "

CHAPTER XII.

"I THINK, Mr. Budd, that Mr. Fenton can give you the advice and counsel that I have so wofully failed to furnish you," remarked Gertrude, after her callers were seated. "You see, Mr. Fenton takes the new woman seriously."

"Surely, Mr. Budd," said John Fenton, "there is no great merit in that. We are obliged to, are we not?"

"I am disappointed in you, Mr. Fenton," exclaimed Gertrude. "I thought you did it willingly, and now you hint at compulsion."

Buchanan Budd grasped the opportunity for a flank movement.

"You have thrown yourself open to suspicion, Mr. Fenton. I fear your counsel and advice to one who is very glad to welcome woman to new privileges would not be as valuable as I had hoped it would be."

Fenton saw that he had placed himself at a disadvantage.

"You both do me an injustice," he explained. "Although there may be, as I have said, no possibility of retreat, we men still take pleasure in advancing with women, rather than against them."

Budd saw at once that his opponent was a strategist worthy of his own Napoleonic skill.

"You see," said Budd, gazing earnestly at Gertrude, "that you find all men ready to capitulate. The burden now lies on your own shoulders. It is for you to direct your allies in the line that they should take."

Gertrude smiled in apparent amusement; but she had a painful consciousness that her hand would tremble perceptibly if she held it out straight before her.

"It seems," she remarked, looking at Fenton, "that everything has been turned around. As a guide and adviser to men, I fear that woman is not yet quite up in her part."

"As my friend Richard Stoughton, — you met him at the musicale last evening, Miss

Van Vleck, — as Stoughton puts it, woman has
evoluted into a mentor from a tormentor," remarked Fenton, proving that he was no longer
a young man, by quoting the witticism of a
friend and giving credit to the author.

"I have been told that Mr. Stoughton is
clever," remarked Gertrude. "He is on a
newspaper, is he not?"

A slight flush mounted to Fenton's cheek.

"Yes," he answered, looking at Budd
steadily; "he is one of my colleagues on the
Trumpet."

"Ah," commented Budd, with what he
doubtless considered an effectively Napoleonic
drawl, "you are — ah — in journalism, Mr.
Fenton?"

There was nothing offensive in the words
themselves, but the speaker's tone implied that
he considered journalism a line of endeavor
that was not recognized in his set. Gertrude
Van Vleck understood the veiled sneer in his
voice, and her eyes shone mischievously as she
cast a rapid glance at Fenton, and then said
to Budd, —

"It seems to me, and I know so many women who agree with me, that journalism is, above all others, the appropriate profession for a man of intellect in these days."

So far as good form permitted it to express any emotion, Buchanan Budd's face wore a look of surprise as she uttered these words. Fenton smiled slightly, and said, —

"Won't you explain your position, Miss Van Vleck? Your remark is so distinctly complimentary to my line of life that I should be delighted to have you enlighten us further regarding your reason for the conclusion you have reached."

"Perhaps that would be killing two birds with one stone," suggested Gertrude enthusiastically. "Mr. Budd has been asking my advice about the best method of getting into touch with the new ideas that are influencing the world — especially as they apply to woman. It seems to me that the life of a newspaper man must, of necessity, place him in sympathy with the most advanced tendencies of thought. I mean, of course, a newspaper man who holds a position of any prominence in journalism."

"If I follow you — ah — Miss Van Vleck," put in Budd, his drawl growing somewhat more pronounced as he realized that the enemy had cleverly thrown him upon the defensive, "if I follow you, the proposition seems to be that in order to become thoroughly imbued with the theories that dominate woman at present, I should — ah — go into journalism."

Gertrude laughed nervously.

"What do you advise, Mr. Fenton? Mr. Budd is honestly anxious to be progressive; he even flattered me by saying that I could help him to overcome certain ancient prejudices that still cling to him. But I feel convinced that you can be of more service to him in this matter than I — or any woman — could ever be."

"I fear," said Fenton coldly, "that the treatment for Mr. Budd, at which you have hinted, is much too heroic. The life of the New York newspaper man is not devoted to the study of theories, but to the discovery and publication of facts. Our effort is to free from imprisonment poor old 'Truth, crushed to earth,' to use the words of the poet."

"I suppose — ah — Mr. Fenton," suggested Budd, "that the reason the newspapers stir up so much mud, then, is that they find — ah — Truth in such an unfortunate position."

Gertrude and Fenton laughed outright.

"Very well put, Mr. Budd," exclaimed the latter. "I feel convinced that you need no outside aid to enable you to keep up with current tendencies; provided, of course," — and Fenton looked earnestly at Budd, — " provided, of course, that you honestly prefer to be progressive rather than reactionary."

Budd had arisen to make his adieux.

"I — ah — feel very much encouraged, Mr. Fenton, by your words. Especially as they don't condemn me — ah — to a newspaper life," he said, smiling sarcastically. Then he turned and took Gertrude's hand.

"I hope, Miss Van Vleck," he said earnestly, "that you feel encouraged about my redemption."

Gertrude looked at him with mock solemnity.

"I fear, Mr. Budd, that the age of miracles has long gone by."

Budd strolled thoughtfully along the avenue toward his favorite club. "She is mistaken about the age of miracles," he was saying to himself. "There are amazing and inexplicable phenomena in sight all around us. A newspaper man who appears to advantage in a drawing-room! Is not that a miracle? And I even suspect that she admires him. It's most incredible."

There was a great deal in the world that astonished Napoleon when he reached St. Helena and had time to sit down and think.

.　　.　　.　　.　　.

"Do you know anything of a man named John Fenton — a journalist, I believe?" asked Buchanan Budd of Percy-Bartlett when he reached the club.

"Yes," answered the latter. "Fenton belonged to our set years ago — before you entered it, you know. He's a thoroughbred, but eccentric, and completely out of the running."

This answer did not tend to restore Budd's disturbed equilibrium. He suspected that Percy-Bartlett underrated John Fenton's staying powers.

CHAPTER XIII.

It was a bright moonlight night as John Fenton strode hurriedly away from the Van Vleck mansion, and bent his steps toward Richard Stoughton's apartments. Just why, at such an hour, he had determined to call on his youthful friend, he could hardly say. He was discontented with himself and the world. He had had, in a certain sense, an enjoyable evening; but a man of Fenton's age and mental tendencies does not make a radical change in his habits without a protest that finds expression in his actions. A broken piston-rod may not ruin an Atlantic liner, but it causes many eccentric variations in the vessel's course.

For ten years past John Fenton had been a man of somewhat questionable habits, and of distinctly iconoclastic convictions. He had discovered, of a sudden, that a change had crept over the details of his daily life, and that his iconoclasm was no longer followed by an exclamation point, but by an interrogation mark. What influence had been brought to bear to beget these changes, he was not sure. He realized that his intercourse with Richard Stoughton had had some effect upon his mode of life and cast of thought, but he had never acknowledged to himself that he had taken the young man *au sérieux*. That a rather superficial boy, not long out of college, could throw a man of Fenton's age and character entirely out of time-worn grooves seemed to be an absurdity. But as Fenton strode down the avenue, so deep in self-communion that he noted not the beauty of the night, he realized that influences he could not trace, and whose force he could not measure, had been at work to disturb the even tenor of his life, and to throw him back into that state of unrest and questioning that had agitated his existence before he had abandoned, as he fondly thought forever, the ambitions that the average man cherishes.

Modern life has one characteristic that must be taken into consideration as we follow the outward manifestations in our fellow-men of the inward impetus that dominates them; namely, its complexity. An individual, in this age of the world, is powerless in any effort to shape his life in opposition to the currents that influence the world at large. Isolation is practically impossible. Our butler remarks that coffee and tea have become expensive luxuries. We realize that a revolution in Brazil, or a war in the far East, has had its effect in swelling the expenses of our cuisine.

Society is closely knit together. Jenkins, the millionnaire, gets drunk at dinner. The butler tells the cook, the cook tells his sweetheart, his sweetheart tells her brother, her brother tells a bartender, the bartender tells a loafer, the loafer tells a tramp. Does not all this illustrate the perfect brotherhood of man?

John Fenton had made a close study of modern social problems; and he was thoroughly conversant with the fact that the interdependence of individuals has been vastly increased by the characteristic features of contemporary life. Nevertheless, there was a certain stubbornness in his make-up that made him revolt against the very tendencies that had seemed to him, in his more optimistic moods, to insure the final salvation of society. He was a man who objected to the idea that he had yielded to an influence that he could not follow to its source, and had drifted away from his former moorings. Accepting the complexity of society as a stimulating, and perhaps encouraging, fact, he objected to its personal application. He had tried hard to be a rebel in manner as well as in theory. That he had sent up a flag of truce was a conviction that filled him with both self-distrust and discontent.

As he turned into the side street leading to Stoughton's lodgings, he stopped before a brilliantly lighted saloon. For fully a month Fenton had abstained almost entirely from alcoholic stimulants; but at this moment he craved the revivifying influence of a cocktail. He turned back into the avenue, and retraced his steps for half a block. He was astonished at his hesitation, — his seemingly childish lack of determination. He tried to analyze his mood. He realized that he had no objections to offer to one harmless little cocktail at ten o'clock at night. What, then, was it that caused him to repass the saloon without entering it? "Perhaps," he said to himself, "perhaps I am growing snobbish again since I returned to the inner circle. If I want a cocktail hereafter I shall be obliged to rejoin one or more of my old clubs."

Fenton found Richard Stoughton still seated before the dying embers of the fire, and thoughtfully puffing cigar-smoke into the heavy atmosphere.

"Come, come, Richard," cried Fenton, throwing up one of the windows. "You might as well go the pace in gay company as to ruin your constitution in solitude in a room actually choking with nicotine. I was not sure that I should find you; but I took the chance."

Richard gazed at his friend searchingly as he handed him a cigar.

"Well, John, I'm glad to see you, of course, although I had not looked forward to your

reappearance to-night.   And now tell me, old
man, are you with us or against us?"

"I don't quite understand your question,
Richard," exclaimed Fenton, regretting for a
moment that he had not taken a cocktail to
restore his nervous energy.

"Well, John, forgive me then, if I take a
liberty and put my question in different words.
Did you enjoy your call on Miss Van Vleck?"

"Those are, indeed, very different words,
Richard.   The two questions seem to have
no very close relationship."

"Perhaps not, John.   That's for me to judge.
But answer one or the other of them; which-
ever one you choose."

"Well, my boy, I can say honestly," remarked Fenton guardedly, "that I have had
a very pleasant evening."

"But it was not wholly satisfactory, or you
wouldn't be here," commented Richard in a
tone of conviction.   "Come, old man, free
your mind.   You need a father-confessor.   I'll
try to fill the *rôle* if you will bear with my
youth and inexperience."

Fenton puffed at his cigar in silence for a time, and gazed moodily into the gleaming coals in the grate.

"I acknowledge, Richard," he said at length, "that I am in a disturbed state of mind. But if I can't help myself, nobody else can give me the aid I need."

"Proud and stubborn heart," cried Richard. "Let me diagnose your case. You believe in certain novel theories, and have become a convert to various economic teachings that embrace more in their ultimate effects than a mere question of taxation. You are suddenly confronted by the fact that it is possible for even political economy to demand martyrs on the altars it has raised. Naturally, you object to being a martyr."

"Your way of putting it, Richard," said Fenton slowly, "may have a basis of truth. I admit that I seem to have come to a turning-point imperatively demanding a decision on my part that will have a radical effect on my life."

"It is," suggested Richard, "a question of hearts *versus* theories."

"Not yet, perhaps," answered Fenton; "but it may become so if I don't call a halt at once in my present methods."

"No man can serve two masters to-day, John, any more than our remote ancestors could when the proposition was first put into words. Of course you know, without any explanation on my part, how my sympathy lies in the struggle that is worrying you. In the first place, although I may be forced to admit the strength of the premises upon which the writer you call master bases his conclusions, I refuse to accept the conclusions. Chasing a rainbow seems to me to be a useless occupation, no matter how much we admire the rainbow. Furthermore, the personal element enters largely into my way of looking at this matter. I have grown very fond of you, John," and Richard's voice grew almost caressing in its tone, "and I should like to see you take the path to happiness that chance has thrown open to you."

"We are talking in the air, my boy," said Fenton earnestly, with a note of sadness in his intonation. "It is only excessive egotism on my part that could lead me to believe that the path to happiness of which you speak has really opened up before me."

"But if," persisted Richard, "you felt sure that by sacrificing what I take the liberty of calling your chimerical efforts to put salt on the tail of the millennium, you could win the joy that has suddenly met your gaze, would you not abandon your philanthropic but hopeless dreams for the alluring reality within your grasp?"

"Frankly, Richard," answered Fenton, after a moment's silence, "I cannot answer the question to-night. It takes a man in middle life a long time to overturn the results of ten years of reading and thinking and endeavor. But I am glad that you have put the problem in concrete form. I can look at it more calmly now that I have heard you put it into words. But it is late and I must go. I have been very selfish, Richard, I fear. Tell me, my boy, why have you wasted an entire evening looking at a bed of coals, and blowing smoke into the air?"

Richard smiled as he took Fenton's outstretched hand.

"I have been trying to come to a decision, John."

"And have you reached it ?"

"I fear not, old man. Decisions are hard to arrive at, John, are they not ?"

"They are, indeed," assented Fenton sadly, as he said good-night.

CHAPTER XIV.

"I SENT for you to cheer me up, Gertrude, but, really, you're the most depressing creature I've seen in a long time. You're not like yourself at all. What is the matter?"

Mrs. Percy-Bartlett and Gertrude Van Vleck were spending an afternoon together, indulging in what the former called "boudoir repentance." Lent had come, and the reaction from social gayety had caused society to sit down for a time and try to think. Sackcloth and ashes were very becoming to Mrs. Percy-Bartlett; for she had never looked more attractive to the eyes of Gertrude Van Vleck than she did at that moment, as she drew her chair close to her friend's side, and, taking her hand, smiled up into her troubled face questioningly.

"You have something on your mind, Gertrude; I am sure of it. Tell me what it is."

Gertrude Van Vleck's clear-cut face was paler than its wont, and there were dark circles under her eyes.

"You are mistaken, Harriet," she answered evasively. "I always feel a certain depression when Lent begins. I suppose that that is very becoming on my part. Lent means more to us, whose days are nearly all Easters, than to people who spend their whole lives in the shadow of self-sacrifice and denial. Do you know, Harriet, I sometimes feel a great pity for the worried and overworked world that lies outside our set. It seems so unjust that a few of us should have all the good things of the earth, while the millions are obliged to toil and sicken and die in the mere effort to get enough to eat and wear."

Mrs. Percy-Bartlett looked at Gertrude with undisguised astonishment in her eyes.

"What queer ideas you are getting into your head, Gertrude! I am glad you are going to Europe so soon. The change will do you good."

"I hope it will, Harriet," said Gertrude earnestly, "for I am really wofully out of sorts. I have often thought, don't you know, that it was a glorious thing that we women of to-day are not contented to take everything for granted, and are inclined to do a little reading and thinking for ourselves. But we pay the penalty for our intellectual emancipation in various ways. Isn't it Byron who says that 'knowledge is sorrow, and he who knows the most must mourn the most.'"

"What a curious girl you are, Gertrude! I didn't know that anybody ever quoted Byron in these days. He's so old-fashioned, is he not? But, Gertrude, I am really worried about you. Surely it isn't our fault if the world is all wrong. What can we do to set things right? Absolutely nothing, my dear. We might as well feel sorry that the Japanese have killed a lot of Chinamen, as to worry about the poverty and distress on the East Side — or is it the West Side — of this great city. I'm sorry, Gertrude, that you aren't literary, or musical, or something of that kind. It's a wonderful thing to have an outlet for just such moods as you

are in.   If it wasn't for my music, I don't know
what I'd do at times.   Something reckless, I'm
afraid."

"No," said Gertrude sadly, "I haven't anything of that kind to help me out.   I sometimes wish that I could write a great novel.
I know, of course, that that sounds absurd,
but I do so want to do something worth
doing."

Mrs. Percy-Bartlett smiled amusedly at her
companion.

"I hope," she said, "that you won't give way
to the temptation, my dear.   But, seriously,
Gertrude, I want you to make me a promise,
a solemn promise, for the sake of your own
happiness."

"What is it?" asked Gertrude, a sad smile
on her face.   "I am in the mood to promise
almost anything."

"Then, Gertrude," said Mrs. Percy-Bartlett,
gently stroking her friend's hand, "then, I
want you to promise me that you will fall in
love."

Gertrude laughed, almost merrily.

"What a strange request, Harriet! I don't see what my word given to you would be worth in such a case." Then her face took on a look of sadness. "I wonder," she said musingly, "if I ought to tell you something. I should like to so much, Harriet, but it doesn't seem to be quite fair."

Mrs. Percy-Bartlett threw her arm around Gertrude's neck, and drew her close to her side.

"You can trust me, Gertrude. Don't you know you can? I knew that you had something to tell me. Whisper it, my dear. What is it?"

Gertrude bent her head close to her confidante's ear.

"Buchanan Budd proposed to me last night, Harriet."

"And you " —

"And I refused him," answered Gertrude, a hysterical break in her voice.

"I am so sorry," said Mrs. Percy-Bartlett caressingly, as she gently stroked Gertrude's luxuriant hair.

The girl's eyes met hers questioningly.

"Sorry, Harriet; sorry that I refused him?"

"No, no, my dear; not that at all. I'm sorry that you had to go through such an ordeal. But, Gertrude, you have something more to tell me — something more important."

Gertrude Van Vleck drew herself up and looked at her friend searchingly

"You are so hard to satisfy, Harriet," she exclaimed at length. "Is it not enough that I have confessed to you that a man proposed to me last night, and that I rejected him. Really, my dear, you must check your awful appetite for gossip."

Mrs. Percy-Bartlett arose, a hurt look on her face.

"I don't wonder, Gertrude, that a good many people fear you. You say very cutting things at times."

"Forgive me, Harriet," cried Gertrude impulsively. "Come, sit down here. I didn't mean to be sarcastic, my dear. That's nice of you. Come close to me. Don't you know, Harriet, that the penitent never tells quite

all that is on her soul, at the confessional?
You mustn't expect too much of me. I'm
only human, you know, my dear. What would
a woman be without her secret? You must
let me have mine, Harriet, and I will not ask
for yours."

Mrs. Percy-Bartlett flushed slightly as her
eyes met Gertrude's.

"Perhaps I was too exacting, Gertrude,"
she said softly. "But I am so anxious to see
you perfectly happy, that I let my wishes get
the better of my discretion. You'll forgive
me, won't you?"

"Anxious to see me perfectly happy," re-
peated Gertrude musingly. "And that seems
to mean, Harriet, that you would like to have
me married."

Mrs. Percy-Bartlett laughed nervously.

"It does appear illogical," she remarked in
a voice that sounded cold and hard, even to
herself. "It is curious how marriage seems
to make every woman a match-maker. I'm
sure that I, for one, can't understand it."

There was silence in the room for several

moments. Gertrude and Harriet understood each other perfectly; but there is always a well-defined limit to frankness between two women, especially when one is married and the other not.

With studied composure, Gertrude asked indifferently, as she rose to go :—

"Have you seen Mr. Stoughton recently, Harriet?"

"Yes, he has called several times."

"And you like him?"

"Very much. He is coming to-night, I believe. We are very good friends.

With an impulsiveness that was not habitual with her, Gertrude bent and kissed her friend on the lips.

"Be careful, Harriet. Be careful," she whispered, and then turned and left the room.

CHAPTER XV.

"You look tired, Mr. Stoughton. You have been working too hard."

Thus said Mrs. Percy-Bartlett to Richard, as her brown eyes rested questioningly on his pale countenance. When a woman frankly comments on a man's appearance to his face it is evident that her friendship for him is on a very firm basis.

"Perhaps so," returned Richard, smiling gratefully. "I sometimes get very tired of pouring water through a sieve; of rolling a stone to the top of a hill every day to find it at the bottom the next morning."

She bent toward him, and looked up into his face earnestly.

"But it must be a glorious privilege, Mr. Stoughton, to feel that what you write is read by thousands and tens of thousands of people; that you are an important part of that great force in modern life, the daily press."

"In one sense," he returned thoughtfully, "it is a satisfaction to know that you are addressing a large audience — an audience that is powerless to hiss you off the stage if it is not pleased with your words. But at its best my editorial work is both ephemeral and anonymous."

She smiled at him sympathizingly.

"I know what is in your mind," she exclaimed. "You desire the recognition and applause of the public. But that is sure to come to you in time. You have great talents, Mr. Stoughton; and — pardon me for saying so — you are young, and can afford to wait."

They were silent for a time, proof positive that their friendship had made great progress. It is not so much what people say to each other as what they conceal from each other, that marks the status of their intercourse. A long silence between a man and woman seated alone together is very eloquent; and its significance is in direct ratio to their mental alertness. There is no dynamic repression in the silence of a stick and a stone; but when the gods on Olympus cease to speak, the earth trembles with apprehension.

"Do you know," remarked Richard at length, "that I have lost something of the ambition that inspired me some months ago? Perhaps I have grown weary of work, or this great city has had a depressing effect upon my aspirations. Whatever may be the reason, however, I find that I no longer build the castles in the air that I raised with so much enthusiasm not long ago. Why is it, do you think?"

He glanced at her searchingly; and, as their eyes met, her cheeks lost something of their color.

"Ambition may sleep, but it never dies, Mr. Stoughton. You are suffering from the reaction of your sudden and remarkable success."

"My success!" he exclaimed. "Yes; I have won one great and gratifying success since I came to New York; and only one."

"And that is?" she asked softly, and with averted eyes.

"I have made you my friend," he said, bending toward her until the perfume of her luxuriant hair thrilled him with vague ecstasy, and the smile on her lips seemed almost a caress.

Suddenly she looked up at him, and in her eyes lay a troubled and beseeching gleam.

"And the price of my friendship — are you willing to pay it?" she asked gently.

"Of course I am!" he exclaimed. "No sacrifice on my part is too great to make in such a cause. Bargains like this one are made in heaven, are they not?"

"She glanced at him with an expression in her eyes that told him he had wounded her. Without a word she arose and walked into the music-room, and he followed her with a repentant look in his face. Seating herself at the piano, she played softly some of the Lenten music she had heard at the afternoon service.

The prayer of a heart-broken world breathed in the sobbing chords. Then the movement changed, and the harmony seemed to promise rest and peace to the weary sons of men. The spirit of the penitential season had been crystallized in sound, and touched the heart as though a voice had whispered from another world.

The music died away, as if the infinite had taken to its breast the tired soul of one who cried aloud, then passed away in peace; and she turned and looked into the face of the youth at at her side.

"Is it not restful?" she asked gently. "How wonderful it is that music should so change our mood and aspirations."

"And you forgive me?" he asked penitently.

She laughed almost gayly.

"Is it not a habit I've fallen into? I am always granting you pardon, am I not? Do you remember, the very first time I met you you were obliged to ask forgiveness for what you said. How many times since then I've pardoned you I can hardly say. You have been very rebellious."

"How could I be otherwise?" he exclaimed, his eyes avoiding hers. "Does the prisoner feel less impatient because of his chains. It is so difficult, is it not, to be civilized?"

"I hardly understand you, Mr. Stoughton," she said, trying hard to speak very coldly.

"'Cursed be the social lies that warp us from the living truth,"

he quoted.

"How thoroughly Tennyson gives expression to the revolt of youth against the shackles that civilization, so called, has thrown around it! I think I know, to my cost, how he felt when he wrote certain lines in 'Locksley Hall.'"

Richard took a few steps up and down the room, and then threw himself into a chair and looked steadfastly at Mrs. Percy-Bartlett. Her face had lost its color, and there were dark shadows beneath her eyes, while a smile of sadness, perhaps of regret, hovered round her mouth.

"I have something to say to you," she remarked, after a moment's silence, her voice low and firm. "You must sit where you are and listen to me attentively. Will you promise me to weigh my words carefully and — and — not misunderstand me?"

He saw that she was essaying a difficult task, and he said gently, —

"I promise ; go on."

"Then," she continued, smiling at him gratefully, "I want to say frankly that I have taken a great deal of pleasure in our friendship. It is hardly necessary, however, to tell you that. I think I have proved it to you in many ways. But the time has come when it rests with you as to what the future shall hold for us. If you are willing to be a true and unselfish friend to me, — to be 'civilized' in the highest sense of the word, — we can go on as we have gone before. But if — if your chains fret you too much, or if there is the slightest danger that you will ever break them, then it is better that we should part. It is so easy for a man to misunderstand a woman — therefore, I am frank with you. Are you not grateful? Don't you thank me ?" There was a note of pleading in her voice.

Richard arose, and moved restlessly up and down the room a moment. Civilization decreed that he should remain seated and suppress all evidences of emotion; but there is a strong vein of savagery in youth, and Richard Stoughton was very young.

"'They also serve who only stand and wait!'" he exclaimed irrelevantly.

Mrs. Percy-Bartlett laughed outright.

"The quotation does you credit in one way, Mr. Stoughton, even if it doesn't seem to be very *àpropos*."

"Perhaps not," he acknowledged, reseating himself. "But somehow it has relieved the situation. At least, let it indicate that I accept your ultimatum."

"If I knew you well enough," commented Mrs. Percy-Bartlett smilingly, "I should say that that sounded rather cross. I hate to think that I have formulated an ultimatum. That seems unwomanly, does it not?"

"I hardly know," he said musingly. "It is hard to tell in these days what is womanly and what is not. A few years ago we would have said that it was unwomanly for a girl to stand before a miscellaneous audience and make a political speech. No one would dare to take that ground now."

Mrs. Percy-Bartlett smiled sympathizingly.

"I am sure," she said, "that you don't approve of the effort of woman to break away from the old restrictions."

"Not altogether," he answered frankly. "I have a strong vein of New England conservatism in my make-up. It revolts against many of the end-of-the-century ideas that are making such progress in this city."

And so they talked on for a time, in a vein that proved the thorough efficacy of Mrs. Percy-Bartlett's ultimatum.

"It is so much better," she said, as she arose to give him her hand at parting, "it is so much better to talk about the 'new woman' than — than " —

"Than the old Adam," he added. "Yes, I agree with you — for the sake of friendship."

"And you are my friend," she cried impulsively, while he still held her hand, suddenly grown cold.

"Yes," he murmured in a muffled tone, bending and kissing the slender fingers in his grasp.

She stood at the entrance to the music-room until she heard the hall-door close. Then she turned, and seated herself at the piano. It was here that Percy-Bartlett found her, idly weaving strange melodies as the night grew old.

"You look pale and tired, dear," he said gently, as he bent and kissed her colorless cheek. "I did not think that you would wait up."

"Is it late?" she asked wearily. "I had lost all track of time."

"I shall be very glad," remarked her husband, seating himself and lighting a cigar, "when my affairs and the nation's are so arranged that I won't be obliged to talk business at night. Has no one been in, Harriet?"

"Yes," she answered in a careless tone, and striking a few soft chords on the instrument; "Mr. Stoughton called, and stayed an hour or so."

Percy-Bartlett flicked the ashes from his cigar impatiently. He was silent for some time, firmly suppressing any feeling of annoyance that her words had caused.

"You find the boy interesting?" he asked coldly.

She looked at him calmly an instant, and then said indifferently, —

"Well — I prefer him to solitude, at least."

Then she arose and said "good-night," leaving Percy-Bartlett to such comfort as he could derive from his thoughts and his tobacco.

CHAPTER XVI.

It was Saturday night at La Ria's. John Fenton and Richard Stoughton were seated side by side near one end of the room, awaiting with true La Rian patience the coming of the soup. No one who is in a hurry ever goes to La Ria's on Saturday night. Impatience is sacrilege in that Bohemian republic that lies under the sidewalk on a down-town street, and draws into its charming boundaries many of the brightest men and most attractive women in the city. La Ria's is both a pleasure and a protest. The pleasure is on the surface, the protest is underneath. The former is what the true La Rian feels, the latter is what he thinks. His presence on Saturday evening in that famous restaurant proves his unwillingness to permit the New World's metropolis to become nothing but a colorless aggregation of very wealthy and very poor citizens. La Ria's

furnishes an outlet both to the rich and poor
for the inherent fondness in men and women
for the picturesque and unconventional.

There is nothing attractive in this low-
ceilinged room, blue with cigarette-smoke even
before the soup is served; but if you ask the
loyal La Rian if he would have the "historic
banquet-hall " — as an enthusiastic reporter
once called it — changed in any important particular, he would look at you in scorn. Raise
the ceiling, decorate the walls, put in mirrors
and gilding and rugs and a costly service, and
the broken-hearted La Rians would file sorrow-
fully out into the night, bewailing the moment
when money had thrown its fatal blight over
the one spot in the city where the millionnaire
sinks into insignificance when he comes to dine
with the poet and the artist and the journalist,
and where, once a week at least, there is "a
feast of reason and a flow of soul."

"There is a fascination about this sort of
thing that is irresistible," whispered Richard
to John Fenton, as he sipped his claret after
the dinner had been fairly started and gazed

around him in delight. He was still young enough and sufficiently unsophisticated to enjoy the glamour of his surroundings without looking beneath the surface, and seeing there the life-tragedies that the actors in the scene before him concealed under the mask of gayety. His eye caught the smiling glance of a dark-haired girl, with classically regular features and a delicately shaped hand, who raised her wine-glass as she returned his smile and seemed to pledge his health with the utmost goodfellow-ship. She sat at a table half-way down the room, and had been laughing and chatting with several men wearing Van Dyke beards, one of whom, Richard learned later, was a famous painter of perfectly innocuous landscapes — a man who looked like Mephistopheles, but said his prayers before retiring.

"Be careful, Richard," remarked Fenton good-naturedly; "she's a beautiful girl, but very dangerous."

The young man glanced up at his friend laughingly.

"You brought me here, John. You are responsible for the consequences."

"Am I my brother's keeper?" asked the elder man solemnly. "You are old enough, Richard, to take care of yourself, I suppose. I wash my hands of the whole affair."

As the dinner progressed, Richard felt an intoxication that had no foundation in wine; for he was not fond of alcoholic stimulants, and drank very sparingly. There was a strange exhilaration in his surroundings that gave him a novel sensation. Of the hundred and more men and women in the room he knew little or nothing; but he could see that among them were those of both sexes whose faces and bearing indicated refinement and high birth. That there were others whose origin was questionable, and who carried with them the stamp of vulgarity, did not alter, but emphasized, the fact that the noble blood of Bohemia was represented before his gaze. After a time he gave up generalizing about his companions, and found his attention concentrated on the girl who had smilingly touched her glass to him. By the time the cheese and coffee had come he was obliged to admit that she possessed the most fascinating face he had yet seen, and that there was something in the glance of her dark eyes more intoxicating than any cordial he had ever sipped. As he lighted a cigarette, and leaned back in his chair to listen to the songs and speeches that Fenton had told him would follow the dessert, he found himself reproaching his own fickleness, but more than ever determined to make the acquaintance of the *jolie Bohemienne.*

"Wine, women, and song !" exclaimed a dignified but genial-looking man, arising at the farther end of the room, as if to crystallize in one effort the scattered elements of good-fellowship begotten by the modest but very eatable dinner, "and the greatest of these is" — He paused, as if waiting for a reply.

"Wine," cried a few; "women," shouted many; and a solitary voice said "song."

Turning instantly to the reckless individual who had declared in favor of song, the toast-master called upon him by name to arise and vindicate his position. Blushing more with annoyance than modesty, a young man stood up

and broke the silence that followed by chant-
ing in a pleasing but untrained voice a ballad
of Rudyard Kipling, set to music by the
singer. A round of applause followed, and
the ice was broken. Songs and stories followed each other in rapid succession.

"It's great!" exclaimed Richard in Fenton's
ear ; and again he raised his glass to the dark-
haired girl, who was puffing a cigarette in a
nonchalant way and smiling cordially, now and
again, as she caught Richard's eye.

The toast-master arose, and, putting up his
hand for silence, said with simple eloquence, —

"The priests and ministers, the bishops and
strolling preachers, have through the ages called
themselves 'divines ;' and, lo ! they stand aside,
and we, the moderns, give that title in our
heart of hearts to the poets, the dramatists,
the weavers of tales that touch the soul, the
wonder-workers in words and thoughts who
have wrought that glorious temple we call lit-
erature. Homer and Plato and Horace and
Shakespeare and Goethe, — these are the true
'divines ;' these are the inspired and anointed

teachers who, making no demands for our reverence and awe, find all the generations bending the knee before them."

He paused for breath, and a round of applause drove the tobacco-smoke against the ceiling.

"With this introduction," he went on, "I will present an old friend of yours, who has written a poem that he has modestly informed me is 'simply great.'"

A shout of laughter greeted this sally, as a tall, slim man with gray hair and a youthful cast of countenance arose. That he was well known and thoroughly liked was proved by the applause that welcomed him.

He stood at the end of the table at which Richard's inamorata was seated; and, as he recited the following poem, he indicated by look and gesture that the dark-haired girl had been its inspiration — by-play that amused his hearers, but filled Richard with a jealousy that was as pronounced as it was unreasonable.

"I call this little effort to amuse you," said the poet, " Prince Spaghetti's Vengeance."

Then he recited, with a good deal of elocutionary cleverness, the following lines : ·

"Not where garish lights are gleaming,
    Not in brilliant banquet-hall,
Not where waiters, silent, solemn,
    Make the gaudy grandeur pall;
Not where wine is so expensive
    That your very thirst seems crime,
And to 'wet your whistle' often
    Is a recklessness sublime;
But for us a quiet corner
    In a side-street, down a stair,
Vive Bohème and *Vive La Ria!*
    Who would be a millionnaire?
Here are brains, served up *en bon mot*,
    Here's spaghetti, piping hot;
Here's a crowd of jolly fellows,
    Well contented with their lot.
Mayhap, as the feast progresses,
    And the wine flows with the wit,
Visions come, and fancy whispers
    'Tis a palace where we sit.
'Tis the palace Macaroni,
    Built in ages long ago
By a count of many titles,
    Where the waves of Tiber flow.
How we got there doesn't matter.
    Maraschino?   Yes — a drop.
Thanks! a little bit of cognac?
    Just a trifle, on the top.
And the palace by the Tiber,
    Where we dine to-night in state,

Here it was Count Macaroni
    Met his most heart-rending fate.
'Twas when Rome was in a ferment,
    As she used to be at times —
Strange how black that ancient city
    Is with undiscovered crimes —
Then it was that Macaroni
    Princess Gorgonzola met —
Yes, methinks your face is like her,
    Seen beyond this cigarette.
Gorgonzola, she was charming,
    Black-eyed maiden, ripe to fall
In the arms of Love, if mother
    Let her get beyond her call.
Macaroni, Gorgonzola,
    They were such a handsome pair
That in strolling by the Tiber
    E'en the boatmen had to stare.
Well, where am I ? In La Ria's ?
    No; Saint Peter knows I'm not.
Just another sip of cognac ?
    Thanks — it reached the very spot.
Well, the Count and Gorgonzola
    By a villain were pursued,
Prince Spaghetti was his title —
    Scion of an evil brood.
Prince Spaghetti loved the maiden
    In a weird and wicked way,
And he swore that Macaroni
    Must forswear the light of day.
Thus he mixed a potent poison
    In a glass of ruby wine —
Yes, I'll light one more perfecto —
    Gad, I think the earth is mine !

> One more little sip of cognac?
>   Thanks, I cannot say thee nay;
> Well — where was I?   Oh, Spaghetti
>   Macaroni meant to slay.
> Did I kill him?   Say, my fair one,
>   You with Gorgonzola's eyes,
> Did I make him drink the poison?
>   Answer — you who were the prize.
> Well, the tale is nearly ended —
>   Strange that I should live to-night,
> Dining in La Ria's with you.
>   Thanks! that cognac's out of sight.'

A roar of delight rewarded the poet's effort; and he reseated himself smilingly, while the dark-eyed maiden at his table — who, by the way, went by the name of " Gorgonzola " ever after — raised her *liqueur* glass, and drank gratefully to the genius who had done what he could to immortalize her beauty.

The hour was growing late, and the jolly diners had begun to disperse.   Fenton was engaged in a discussion of the single-tax theory with an English newspaper correspondent on his left, when Richard noticed with regret that his inamorata and her friends, the artists, had arisen to take their departure.   It was time for decisive action; and impulsively he fumbled in his cardcase, found his pencil in time to write his address on one of his pasteboards, and had resumed a position of becoming dignity before the gay group, making for the entrance, had reached his table. As the girl passed him, smiling down at him with her dancing black eyes, he handed the card to her. It was all over in a moment, and Richard found himself practically alone. The room seemed utterly deserted after her departure.

"Well, young light-o'-love," remarked Fenton, as they strolled homeward, "have you had a pleasant evening?"

"Delightful,· John," answered the youth. Then he said earnestly, —

"John, at what age do you think that it is possible for a man to fall honestly and thoroughly in love?"

"Not until after he is forty, my boy," answered Fenton gravely. "Don't take yourself or anybody else too seriously, Richard, until you have reached middle life."

"That's not the doctrine you preached to me

some months ago, John Fenton," said Richard thoughtfully.

"I know you better now, my dear fellow," returned Fenton, adding to himself, "and myself too."

CHAPTER XVII.

THAT John Fenton was in a peculiar frame of mind was sufficiently proved by the fact that Sunday morning had arrived, and he had arisen early, — very early, three hours before noon, — and was pleased at this innovation in his habits. It was a clear, bracing day, with a promise of spring in the air, and a saline odor in the breeze, a public confession that it had kissed the sea when the sun came up. How much he owes to the salt air for the sprightliness that is in him the average New Yorker seldom realizes. Manhattan Island is a natural health-resort. That many of its inhabitants languish and die before their time is the fault not of nature but of man.

John Fenton strode down the avenue after breakfast, one of the best-dressed men abroad at that early hour. The last few months had made a great change in his outward appearance. Somewhat to his surprise, he had found that by refraining from alcoholic self-indulgence he had not only gained in nervous energy, but had reaped a fat financial harvest. Renewing his youth in more ways than one, he had expended at his tailor's money that, under his former habits of life, would have gone to swell a saloon's growing surplus. He had been noted in the old days for his good taste in dress, and his years of carelessness had not destroyed his natural ability to select attire that was at once fashionable and becoming.

With a clean-shaven face, a glow on his cheeks, and the light of physical contentment in his eyes, John Fenton looked positively handsome as he entered Richard Stoughton's rooms, and found his young friend, *en négligé*, smoking a pipe, and perusing, with a sense of self-satisfaction that age cannot wither nor custom stale, his work of the previous day as it appeared in print in that morning's edition of the *Trumpet*.

"What is it I see before me?" cried Richard, springing up, and holding out his hand to his guest. "Upon what meat doth this, our Cæsar, feed, that he gets up and out before noon?"

Fenton seated himself, and lighted a cigar.

"Do you know, my boy," he remarked quietly, "I have spent the night in a sleepless vigil, pondering the error of your ways. I have become convinced that it is absolutely imperative that you should be given an antidote for last night's poison."

"I did smoke too much, I acknowledge," returned Richard densely; "but I have drunk several cups of coffee this morning, and feel much better."

"Flippant youngster! have you no reverence in your make-up? I referred not to the cigars, but to the *tout ensemble*."

"Is that her name, John? It's a queer one, you must admit. But, seriously, what are you driving at? Here you are at ten o'clock on Sunday morning — an hour that has for years, as you have told me, found you sound asleep — abroad in the land, dressed with the most extreme care, and delivering sermons gratis to your friends. I acknowledge that there is a mystery here that I cannot solve."

"It is simple enough, Richard. I have come to an important decision, and I am about to take a step in which I want your companionship and sympathy."

There was a solemnity in Fenton's manner that caused Richard to look at him with mingled curiosity and surprise.

"Of course, John, I'll give you all the help I can. But frankly, now, what are you going to do?"

Fenton puffed in silence for a moment, gazing earnestly at his companion.

"What am I going to do, Richard? I'm going to church."

Richard laughed merrily.

"And you want my support and countenance in this heroic purpose? Well, John, I see no reason why I should discourage your eccentric but praiseworthy design. If you'll amuse yourself with the papers for a few moments, I will get into a garb of a more devotional character than this old smoking-jacket. To go to church with John Fenton! That is a privilege that I had never hoped to win. But I've given up all hope of understanding you, John. You're a puzzle I can't solve."

With these words Richard entered an inner room, and left John Fenton to puff his cigar, and glance indifferently over the newspapers. It is seldom that a true journalist cannot find occupation, even excitement, in the latest edition of the newspaper with which he is connected; but, for some reason or other, Fenton was in no mood to take his usual professional interest in the Sunday make-up of the *Trumpet*, and when Richard returned to the room he found his friend standing at the window, and gazing dreamily into the street.

A quarter of an hour later the two friends were seated in one of the rear pews of a church that had kept pace with the demands that the modern love of luxury makes on the outward and visible signs of an inward and spiritual cult. An agnostic, even an atheist, would have felt a reverential awe in such surroundings, an inclination to worship something, if it was nothing but the beauty of interior decoration, as an abstract influence, or the concrete glory of well-dressed women. There is something for all men in a church that frowns not on the æsthetic pleasures that the eye and ear can taste.

As they rose at the opening words of the service, " The Lord is in his holy temple, let all the earth keep silence before him," Richard's eye followed Fenton's, and a new light broke upon his mind. His friend was not as inexplicably eccentric as he had considered him. About half-way between them and the altar, and at an angle that placed her in full view from where they stood; Richard saw Gertrude Van Vleck, a striking figure even in that gathering of women of fashion. He turned on the instant, and his eyes looked into Fenton's. He could not repress a smile that impressed its meaning upon the latter, whose face bore an expression of mingled satisfaction and annoyance as he knelt to join in the general confession. His satisfaction was caused by the

fact that he could watch Gertrude Van Vleck,
unobserved by her, for an entire morning. His
annoyance was due to the mocking light in
Richard's glance.

As the service progressed, with its stately
and impressive words and forms, Richard felt
keenly the influence of his surroundings. He
had been brought up in the atmosphere of the
church, and under its caress the highest dreams
and aspirations of his early youth were revivi-
fied. Before long he had forgotten John Fenton and Gertrude Van Vleck ; and as the soft
strains of Lenten music stole through the per-
fumed air, the face of a brown-eyed woman
whose gaze was sad and tearful filled his soul
with remorse. He felt like one who had committed sacrilege. The garish glitter, the taw-
dry brilliancy, of the night he had spent in
Bohemia seemed to him at that moment piti-
fully repulsive. The dark face of the girl who
had fascinated him for the moment told its true
story as he recalled it in the calm and holy precincts of the temple where he sat. That he
had yielded to the debasing influence that she

had exerted at the time was a fact that filled him with amazement and discontent.

"What strange coincidence is this?" he exclaimed to himself, as the words of the Epistle for the Third Sunday in Lent seemed to voice the thoughts that were surging through his brain: "Be ye therefore followers of God, as dear children; and walk in love, as Christ also hath loved us, and hath given himself for us an offering and a sacrifice to God for a sweet-smelling savour. But all uncleanness, let it not be once named amongst you, as becometh saints; neither foolish talking, nor jesting, which are not convenient: but rather giving of thanks. Have no fellowship with the unfruitful works of darkness, but rather reprove them. For it is a shame even to speak of those things which are done of them in secret."

Richard Stoughton was of an extremely impressionable temperament, and time had not yet hardened the shell that surrounds the soul. It seemed to him at that moment as though the inspired word of God had spoken to him alone in that consecrated temple, and had warned him to seek higher things; to avoid, for the sake of a great reward, the mud-holes and pitfalls in the path before him. He knelt in prayer with a reverential fervor that was new to him.

From the Gospel for the day, St. Luke xi. 14, the rector had taken his text : "He that is not with me is against me ; and he that gathereth not with me scattereth." Richard listened to the sermon with an interest that was almost painful. The preacher was a man not yet in middle life, who had already won a high posi-tion for his eloquence and fearlessness. There was no prosy reiteration of self-evident truths that have lost their influence through long service in the pulpit in the words that he poured forth. He was a man of the times ; and he applied the faith that was in him to the topics of the hour, and drove his lesson home with a skill and courage that were in-tensely effective. He seemed to recognize that he was a warrior in the front ranks of the church militant, and there was no half-heartedness in the blows that he struck. The prosperity of a sermon, like that of a jest, lies in the ear of him that hears it. Richard Stoughton was in a receptive mood, and the ringing words of the preacher touched chords in his nature that had long ceased to vibrate. He bent his head at the benediction with a sense of renewed reverence and faith that was both welcome and inspiring.

When or how he lost track of John Fenton he never knew. He remembered, later on, that as he had left the church he had caught a glimpse of his friend walking down the avenue by the side of Gertrude Van Vleck, but at the moment the sight had made no impression on him. The dominant thought in his mind found expression in the words that seemed to rise uncontrollably to his lips :—

"Forgive us our trespasses, as we forgive those who trespass against us. And lead us not into temptation, but deliver us from evil : For thine is the kingdom, and the power, and the glory, forever and ever. Amen."

CHAPTER XVIII.

IT was a cold night in early spring. It seemed as if the winter had forgotten something, and had returned to look for it. Its search being futile, it had relieved its feelings by howling up and down the streets, feebly tweaking the noses of pedestrians in its senile disappointment.

As an atmospheric crazy-quilt, early spring in New York is a success. The modern craving for variety is fully satisfied in the metropolis, so far as the weather is concerned, from the last of February to the first of June. Between those dates no New Yorker is astonished at anything that may be hurled at him from the skies, from a sunstroke to a blizzard.

John Fenton had had a fire lighted in his grate, and was puffing his after-dinner cigar before the blaze, bewailing inwardly the fact that he was due at the office of the *Trumpet* within the hour.   He would have preferred to spend the evening revising his general theories of life than in correcting proofs at high pressure in the overwrought atmosphere of a newspaper office.

He had much to think about and a weighty decision to make.   He had been drifting in a current that had carried him far in a direction that he had long ago determined never to take again.   For the moment, he could not say whether he was happy or discontented.   For the first time in his life, as he fully realized, he was thoroughly in love ; but, as he pondered the situation calmly, there seemed to be insuperable obstacles in the path that led toward happiness.

"What am I, after all, Richard?" he said to his friend, as Stoughton entered the room and quietly seated himself at the opposite side of the fireplace.   "A wreck that has been patched up ; a failure, not quite hopeless ; a man who has been condemned by the world, with a recommendation to mercy."

"I don't like your mood, John," remarked

Richard, lighting a cigarette, and puffing the smoke slowly into the air. "No game is lost until the hand is played out. I think you stand to win, if you don't lose your pluck. I had good news for you to-day."

"No? What was it?" asked Fenton, with no great show of interest.

"When I reached the office this morning," continued Richard, unawed by his friend's coldness, "I found two letters and a bundle on my desk."

"Yes?"

"One of the letters was from the dark-eyed girl I saw at La Ria's."

Fenton smiled, but said nothing.

"I tore it up, John. I suppose you will call me very young — your pet accusation."

"Hardly, my boy, hardly. You have simply proved that you are wiser in the morning than you are at night."

"Well, most men are, I suppose. There is nothing eccentric or meritorious in that. And so much for 'Gorgonzola.' Let her rest in peace. But the other letter, John, was of more importance. It will interest you."

"Yes?"

"You see, old man, I have played you false. I have come here to confess and to ask forgiveness. You remember you gave me the manuscript of 'Ephemeræ' to read. Well, I took it to a well-known publisher, suppressing the name of the author, and asking for an expression of opinion regarding its merits."

Fenton knocked the ashes from his cigar with a gesture of annoyance, but said nothing.

"Have you no curiosity, John?" exclaimed Richard impatiently. "Don't you care to hear the verdict?"

Without waiting for a reply the youth arose, and, fumbling in his overcoat for a moment, took therefrom a roll of manuscript and a letter.

"I am tempted to punish your indifference, John; but the game is not worth the candle, I fear. Never mind a light. The letter is short. I can read it by the fire, if you will deign to listen. The publisher, John, expresses himself as much pleased with the book, and is inclined to think that it would find a ready market. He objects, however, to the title, and to one or two small details in the *dénoucment*. If you will make the changes he suggests, however, he will bring out the story at once. In closing he politely hints that a type-written copy be returned to him."

Fenton puffed on in silence for a time, and then leaned forward and took the roll of manuscript from Richard's hand. Hesitating an instant, as if to make sure that the decision he had reached was irrevocable, he threw the bundle of paper into the fire. Richard sprang forward, but Fenton seized him by the arm and forced him back into his seat.

"Let it burn, Richard. Let it burn. It has had two narrow escapes from publication already. It shall never have another."

"But are you mad, John? The story would make you famous. Good Heavens, man! it is too late. I call it a crime, John, a crime! Do you hear?"

"Come, come, Richard! don't grow hysteri-

cal," remarked Fenton calmly, as he leaned
back in his chair and resumed his cigar, to dissipate the odor of burnt paper that filled the
room.

"But why, John, did you do such a reckless
thing? You're the last man in the world to
act like a child."

Fenton remained silent for some moments,
and then said gently, —

"We can't hark back in this life, Richard.
Time is an inexorable tyrant. If you try to
take a liberty with him you are certain to be
punished. What I wrote in my youth would
do no credit to my maturity — no matter what
you or a publisher or the public might say
to the contrary. One of the strangest things
about the life of an intellectual man, Richard,
is that his views regarding the fundamental
problems of existence are in a constant state
of change. How we regard death and love and
friendship and immortality, and other matters
of more or less significance, at twenty-five has
little, if anything, to do with the way we look
at these matters twenty years later. I know

of no greater wrong you could do to a man of intelligence than to present to him in type a record of the opinions he openly expressed ten years ago, and inform him that it was imperative that he should go before the public on that basis. In fact, Richard, I have grown very suspicious of those chameleons we so proudly call convictions. Lucky is the man who can reach middle life and still feel absolutely certain that two and two make four."

Richard remained silent for a time after Fenton had ceased to speak, but finally said gently, —

"I think, John, that I can see as much through a knot-hole as most men of my age, when the points of interest are called to my attention; but I must acknowledge that I had never expected to hear you preach the doctrine of uncertainty."

"You mistake me, boy. I preach nothing!" exclaimed Fenton, arising and peering at his watch in the darkness. "Nothing but the glorious doctrine that hard work is the only relief from futile questionings. Good-night, my boy. I am sorry to rush off, but I must get to the office at once. And you?"

"Can't you guess?" asked Richard, smiling.

"I might if I tried," answered Fenton, holding his friend's hand a moment; "but I sha'n't try. But bear in mind, Richard, that the glory of a renunciation lies in the strength of the temptation."

"I thought, John, that you had no convictions!" exclaimed Richard pointedly.

"You are mistaken, boy," returned Fenton, with a touch of his old cynicism. "Every man has a large supply of them — to offer to his friends. Good-night."

CHAPTER XIX.

"You are very thoughtful, Mr. Stoughton," remarked Mrs. Percy-Bartlett gently, as she wheeled around on the piano-stool and looked Richard squarely in the face.

"I was weighing a sentence just uttered by John Fenton — one of those haunting phrases of his that will not take a back seat when they have once entered the mind."

"He must be a man of peculiar power, this John Fenton," commented Mrs. Percy-Bartlett musingly. "I have heard him quoted a good deal of late."

"By Gertrude Van Vleck?" asked Richard, with an impulsive exhibition of bad taste.

Mrs. Percy-Bartlett frowned.

"I am astonished, Mr. Stoughton! Your question is simply shocking. But tell me," she continued, leaning forward, and looking at him inquisitively, "do you really think that Mr. Fenton is interested in Gertrude?"

"I am astonished!" cried Richard. "Your question is simply shocking, Mrs. Percy-Bartlett."

Their eyes met, and they laughed merrily. They were both very happy for the moment. The love-affairs of other people may form at times a very effective counter-irritant and delay a crisis that Platonic friendship is apt to carry with it when a young married woman and an ardent youth use it as a cloak to conceal their feelings.

"In some respects," remarked Mrs. Percy-Bartlett musingly, "it would be an ideal union."

"If there are such," put in Richard reflectively.

"That sounds like the cynicism of your friend Mr. Fenton. I hope, Mr. Stoughton, that you are not losing your ideals."

"On the contrary," said Richard earnestly, "I am finding new ones."

"May I ask where?" she murmured, a wistful look in her brown eyes.

"I have found the highest of them all in this

little music-room," he said with more earnestness in his tone than it had held before. "What ideal is so beautiful as that which forms the basis of our friendship? Is it not true that the altar on which we make the hardest sacrifice is that which becomes the most sacred in our sight? I might live a thousand years, but when memory grew weary of its heavy task, it would still turn fondly to the scene before me now, and I would see myself in fancy a youth with an ideal — an ideal that sealed his lips — and broke his heart."

He had turned very pale, and his words seemed to him to have been forced from him by a mysterious and irresistible influence that he could neither recognize nor control.

The woman's eyes were heavy with unshed tears. As he had gone on speaking in a low, vibrant tone, she had felt the blood rush to her face, and then recede, leaving her cheeks white and drawn. Her hands trembled as she turned and struck a few wavering, melancholy chords on the piano.

Richard had arisen, and was looking down at

her, his face grown old, as if life had whispered
a mighty secret into his unwilling ears, and
marred the pristine glory of his youth.

Neither of them spoke for a time. Finally
he said, —

"I had started to quote to you something
that Fenton said. Do you care to hear it?"

His voice was almost hard with the effort
he made to control its trembling.

"Yes," she murmured, looking up at him,
in her eyes a mute appeal, an unspoken prayer
to his nobler self.

"'The glory of a renunciation,' said my
friend, 'lies in the strength of the temptation.'"

She put her cold, trembling hand into his
and their eyes met.

"Please go," she whispered. "If you care
for me at all you will do as I ask."

She withdrew her hand, and Richard turned
away as if determined to do as she had
requested. For a moment he saw himself in
his true character, — an impressionable, impetuous man, inexperienced in the ways of the

world, and easily influenced by his surroundings. He saw himself casting meaning glances at a dark-eyed girl in an unconventional restaurant. Then the remorse and self-loathing that had come over him as he knelt in prayer in the sombre shadows that haunted a church-pew returned for an instant, and he felt an irresistible desire to prove, for his own satisfaction, that the higher aspirations that had dominated him later on were not mere fleeting fancies. He turned and reseated himself in the chair at her side.

"Forgive me for what I've said," he implored, his voice low and firm; "I dare not leave you now. It will drive me mad to reflect that I have been unkind to you. I have been very selfish. Let me have at least one more chance to prove that I can be your friend."

She smiled sadly, and turning to the instrument played softly the refrain of Heine's melancholy song.

The impotence of longing, the futility of rebellion, were emphasized in Richard's restless mind as he recalled the words of the poem

she had set to music. What availed it that
the pine-tree craved the palm? The inexorable fiat of a universe controlled by laws as
pitiless as they are unchangeable had decreed
that only in dreams should its love find satisfaction.

She turned and looked at him again. Her
face was pale, and there were shadows beneath
her eyes, but in her smile was a ray of
sunshine.

"Why can you not be content?" she asked
gently. "Do you not find pleasure in spending an evening with me now and then?"

"You need not ask," he murmured.

"But do you know that it would end all
this if — if " —

"If?"

"If you were always as reckless as you have
been to-night."

"How hard it is to obtain justice in this
world," he cried, a faint smile on his lips.
"How well I know that, far from being reckless, I have exercised the greatest self-restraint.
Do you know, — please don't turn your eyes

away, — do you know what temptation I have resisted to-night? Is it not true that the grandeur of a victory lies in the martial power of the enemy overthrown? I would have been a coward had I retreated when you asked me to. Is it not better for us to sit here contentedly and talk of friendship?"

She glanced at him deprecatingly.

"Do you know," she said in a tone of sadness, "that there is sometimes a mocking note in your voice and an expression on your face that make me wonder if you ever take yourself or any one else seriously?"

She had put into words a doubt that had never before been symbolized in his mind, though often vaguely felt. He was silent for a moment, wondering if it was only his youth, or a fundamental defect in character, that had awakened in her a questioning that found so unwelcome a response in his own heart. Unfortunate is that man who finds nothing at the very depths of his own personality but an interrogation mark.

"Are you not unreasonable?" he suggested

quietly, striving to obtain self-justification. "When I speak earnestly — and honestly — you ask me to leave you. When I openly ratify the terms upon which you allow me to remain, you say I jest. I almost despair of ever winning your favor."

She smiled encouragingly.

"I like you now," she remarked frankly. "Perhaps, after all, I am not as daring a rebel as I once told you that I was."

Some one had entered the drawing-room; and turning toward the portière, they saw Percy-Bartlett, his pale face just a shade whiter than usual.

"Good-evening, Stoughton," he said, coming forward and giving the young man his hand. "Harriet, we ask your indulgence. Shall we smoke here or go into the library?"

Richard's first inclination was to take his departure at once, but he realized in time the awkwardness that would attend such a step.

"Always the slaves to habit!" cried Mrs. Percy-Bartlett, with a vivacity born of nervous reaction rather than of satisfaction at the *contretemps*.

"I long ago gave up the idea of defending my music-room from cigar-smoke, Mr. Stoughton. In fact, I have become fond of it. I think," and she looked at her husband smilingly, but with a gleam of defiance in her eyes, "that I will take to cigarettes. They're really quite good form in these days, are they not?"

"It is hard to say at present," remarked Percy-Bartlett, puffing his cigar reflectively, "what is good form and what is not. I confess, Stoughton, that I am rather old-fashioned in my ideas."

"For instance?" suggested Richard, not wholly at his ease.

"There are a thousand illustrations on my tongue. But of what use is resistance? The new ideas — and cigarettes are an appropriate symbol of many of them — are too strong at present in their initial force to succumb to opposition. But I have never lost faith in the power of reaction. We have gone ahead too fast. There must be a return to the old ways soon."

Mrs. Percy-Bartlett turned restlessly to the piano, and struck a few defiant chords on the instrument. She had expressed a doubt as to her status as a rebel. Her husband had appeared at the right moment to fling those doubts to the wind.

As Richard arose to take his departure, Percy-Bartlett said to him, with more cordiality than the young man inwardly felt that he deserved from such a source, —

"Don't let the atmosphere in which you are thrown, Stoughton, cause you to cast away your birthright. It is on men of birth and education that the safety of this country ultimately depends. You should be — and I hope you are — a conservative of the conservative. I want to get you into the Sons of the Revolution and the Society of Colonial Wars. I am an enthusiast on these things, Stoughton, — a man must have a fad, you know, — and you're the kind of material that we can't afford to give to the enemy. Good-night! Drop into my office some morning soon, and we'll talk these matters over."

Mrs. Percy-Bartlett gave her cold hand to Richard and said, with a conventional intonation that chilled him, in spite of the soft expression in her eyes, —

"And we will see you soon again, Mr. Stoughton?"

"Thanks," he said, "and good-night."

Percy-Bartlett had reseated himself, and was taking the final puffs from his cigar, as his wife returned and began to rearrange the sheets of music on the piano.

"Stoughton is a boy I think I might like," remarked Percy-Bartlett, gazing at his wife steadily. "But he looks worn-out. I fear he is overdoing things."

"Perhaps," she answered with studied indifference. "I suppose his work is very wearing."

"Yes; and that's what I can't understand about the youngster. He has money of his own. Why doesn't he travel and study instead of tying himself to such a merciless mill-wheel as a daily newspaper?"

How magnificent is man's blind egotism!

Percy-Bartlett, a millionnaire, was devoting his whole time and nervous energy to adding to his wealth, and still he censured a youth, by no means rich, for following a line of life that insured him a living. It is so easy to demand of our neighbor that he lead an ideal existence!

"You look very pale, my dear," remarked his wife after a long silence, with more concern in her voice than it often held in his hearing.

"I am not feeling especially well," he returned gratefully, and throwing away his cigar, "I must give up smoking, Harriet. The doctor says it is imperative."

CHAPTER XX.

JOHN FENTON had once called Mr. Robinson, of the *Trumpet*, an argus-eyed editor. But Fenton did not fully realize how searching and far-reaching was his superior's gaze. The managing editor of a New York newspaper is seldom appreciated at his true worth by his subordinates. They are too closely in touch with the methods by which he produces his effects to grant him that admiration that the readers of his newspaper feel for him. It is enough if the navigator of a journalistic craft obtains the respect and loyalty of his crew. He must not expect to be the object of hero-worship in the forecastle. It depends upon which end of the telescope you place before your eye, the impression that the moon makes on your mind. The public looks at a famous editor through the large end of the instrument, while his subordinates view him

through the small end.   Rare and precious
is the newspaper potentate who can stand
both tests.

Editor Robinson of the *Trumpet* was not
a great man, — a creature that the end of
the century seems disinclined to produce in
any line of human endeavor, — but he possessed ripe experience, a wide range of vision,
and a keen appreciation of the merits and
demerits of the material at his disposal.   In
judging the availability of a piece of news or
the advisability of a certain line of editorial
policy his mind worked with great rapidity
and acuteness.   When it came to rendering
a final verdict regarding any man with whom
he came in contact he was hesitating and
conservative.   He had learned by experience
that it is dangerous to admire Dr. Jekyll too
much until you have proved conclusively that
he is not a Mr. Hyde.

There were two men in the office who had,
of late, been under Mr. Robinson's close in-
spection.   He was making a thorough study
of John Fenton and Richard Stoughton for

a cherished purpose that he had long had at heart. Many circumstances had combined to lead him to the conclusion that slowly but surely these two men had rendered themselves eligible for a post that neither of them had ever dreamed of filling.

A man is always going up or coming down in a newspaper office, — a fact that proves how like the world at large a journalistic sanctum is. In Mr. Robinson's eyes, Fenton and Stoughton were on the up-grade. Regarding Fenton he had long been in doubt. He had grown to look upon him as a man of ability who had lost all ambition, and whose questionable habits and iconoclastic tendencies of thought had unfitted him for any higher place than he already held. Fenton's long service in the city department and his thorough knowledge of men and affairs in the metropolis had rendered him a valuable assistant, in spite of his peccadilloes and theories; but that he would ever become fitted for a higher line of journalistic achievement Mr. Robinson had never imagined. For some months, however,

the managing editor's keen eye had observed
a great change in Fenton's demeanor and appearance. Much to Mr. Robinson's astonishment, he saw that his subordinate was inclined
to refrain from alcoholic stimulants, that he
had grown very particular about his attire
and that he seemed fond of the society of
young Stoughton.

Mr. Robinson was what the world calls a
self-made man. He had "come up from the
case," as the expression goes, having been a
journeyman printer in the days of his youth.
It is a curious fact that a man who has
made a success of his life in spite of heavy
obstacles can never destroy a certain unde-
fined admiration for a man who, being born
to wealth, position, and leisure has carelessly
thrown away his advantages and fallen from
his high estate. The fact that Fenton had
abandoned as useless toys the very things for
which Robinson had been striving all his life
gave the city editor, — as Fenton was at this
time, — a unique place in the eyes of his chief.
In his heart of hearts, he considered Fenton

a being superior to himself; and it was this feeling that often added a brusqueness to his manner when dealing with his subordinate that had not tended to make their relations very cordial. But, then, cordiality between the heads of the various departments of a metropolitan daily is a gem as rare as it is precious. Down in the pressroom a great object-lesson is presented to the eyes of a thoughtful man. Here is a vast amount of machinery, the most insignificant part of which is obliged to work in perfect union with all other parts, small or great. By the constant application of oil, friction is prevented and the gigantic presses perform their task in a way that shows what tremendous results can be obtained by a complicated machine when absolute sympathy between all the varying features is maintained.

How different is the working of the great brain-engine above stairs! Here man rubs against man, jealousy and discontent and favoritism do what they can to clog the machinery; and the more one knows about the inner life of a newspaper-office, the more the wonder grows that the newspaper of to-day approximates so closely to the highest journalistic ideal. You may find flaws, gentle reader, in what your favorite journal says, but its typographical make-up is always perfect. Bear in mind that the brain-machine that turns out the ideas it presents is laboring under the obstacles that poor, weak, erring human nature begets, while the engines that deal with the materialistic make-up of the paper are influenced neither by jealousy nor heart-burning, neither by revenge nor malice. If the harmony that prevails in the workings of the press-room could dominate the editorial departments, an ideal newspaper would be the result — a result that will not be obtained until the millennium has done its elevating work.

It is just possible that Mr. Robinson was not altogether at ease in his mind over the advance that John Fenton had made in his outward bearing and in his position and influence on the *Trumpet*. One of the chief occupations of an editor in charge of a great

newspaper consists in keeping his mind awake
to possible rivals. That Fenton had become
in the last few months a very important factor in the office was apparent to the most insignificant reporter; and to Mr. Robinson the
desirability of checking the rise of a possible
competitor seemed imperative. But hard steel
or cold poison is not available in these days
for the removal of a man who stands in our
way. In a newspaper-office, however, there
are weapons that take their place. One is
promotion, the other is exile. In the case of
John Fenton, Mr. Robinson had decided, after
mature consideration, to combine both.

"I have sent for you, Mr. Fenton," remarked the editor, smiling cordially as he
wheeled around in his chair and motioned to
his subordinate to be seated, "to discuss quite
an important matter."

"*Timeo Danaos, et dona ferentes*," muttered
Fenton to himself, as he drew up a chair and
looked at his chief inquiringly.

"Pardon me, I didn't catch your remark?"
and Mr. Robinson looked at Fenton suspiciously.

"I am at your service Mr. Robinson, "I said," answered Fenton, smiling.

"Ah, very good of you! Well, now tell me, Mr. Fenton, what is your opinion of young Stoughton? You have seen a great deal of him, have you not?"

"Yes; he's a very clever boy. I'm exceedingly fond of him."

"You find him thoroughly companionable?"

"Extremely so," answered Fenton, wondering what the editor was getting at. Mr. Robinson did not waste time in the afternoon on unimportant gossip.

"And now, Mr. Fenton," continued Robinson, putting the tips of his fingers together, after a habit that pertained to his more Machiavellian moods, "how long is it since you were on the other side?"

"Fifteen years, I think," answered Fenton reflectively. "I spent two years in London and on the Continent just before I went into newspaper work."

"Hum! Very good. Well, the fact is, Mr. Fenton, I have long had a scheme in mind for

making a great improvement in our foreign
service. Stilson, you know, has resigned the
London office. My idea is this: I am very
much pleased with young Stoughton's work as
a paragrapher. He's very pithy, and his style
has really created quite a sensation. Now,
there is no man in the profession who has
a more artistic estimate of news than you
have, Mr. Fenton. Furthermore, your acquaintanceship with men and affairs has been wide,
and, I might say, international. It seems to
me that if you took the London office, with
Stoughton as your assistant, we could make
a great feature of a line of news-matter in
which we have been pretty weak of late years.
You catch my idea ? You're to shoot the
game, and Stoughton's to dress it for the table.
I needn't tell you, of course, that your salary
will be much larger in London than it is here,
and the work will be much easier and of a
character more acceptable to your tastes, Mr.
Fenton."

John Fenton's mind had been very busy
while Mr. Robinson was speaking. Three

months before he would not have hesitated
a moment to accept the editor's proposition.
He was not sure now that it did not offer a
solution to a difficulty that he had not yet had
strength of mind enough to solve himself.
But Fenton was not a man to do anything in
a hurry — unless it was to fall in love. He
looked at Mr. Robinson in silence for a moment, and then said, —

"There is much that is very satisfactory
to me in what you have said, Mr. Robinson.
But I'm a slow, rather conservative man, and I
seldom come to a conclusion in a hurry. May
I have a day or two to weigh this matter?"

"Oh, certainly, certainly," answered the
editor, not wholly pleased at the position
Fenton had taken. "Give me your answer
day after to-morrow. It will do as well then
as now."

Fenton arose to go.

"And about Stoughton?" he asked.

Mr. Robinson sat silent for a time. Finally
he said, —

"I leave him to you, Mr. Fenton. Talk the

matter over with him, and bring him with you when you come to me Monday. Good-day."

Fenton returned to his desk in a more excited mood than he had expected ever to feel again. When a man renews his youth the rejuvenation is apt to bring with it many surprises. That it should make any important difference to him whether he lived in New York or London was an astonishing fact to John Fenton. It was an unpleasant truth that, in a way, forced him to come to a decision that he had been avoiding for a long time. Should he or should he not give up all thought of making Gertrude Van Vleck his wife, was the question that haunted him.

And Mr. Robinson, gazing moodily out of the window in his room up-stairs, was thinking that John Fenton's hesitation was due to ambition.

CHAPTER XXI.

"IF we go, Richard, we burn our bridges behind us."

So said John Fenton, as he walked restlessly up and down the room, puffing a pipe nervously, his face paler than usual, and a gleam in his eyes that indicated a mind disturbed.

Stoughton was lounging in one of Fenton's easy-chairs and gazing at his friend questioningly. It was the evening of the day on which Fenton had listened to Mr. Robinson's proposition, and he had summoned Richard to his rooms for a council of war.

"I am fully convinced," continued Fenton, "that the best thing that could happen to you at present, Richard, would be a long absence from New York. As for myself, I am not sure that this London scheme would not save me from making a fool of myself. But " —

"But," put in Richard solemnly, "you love

Gertrude Van Vleck. The 'but' is a very important one. Why should you give her up? Of course, John, there are several reasons why I can see an advantage for myself in going to London as your assistant. But I am perfectly willing to waive all that, if you'll throw away your unreasonable scruples, and take the good the gods provide."

Fenton seated himself and puffed at his pipe musingly.

"There's a vulgar assertion," he remarked at length, " that informs us how hard it is to teach an old dog new tricks. Admitting, Richard, that what you say is true, — granting your premises, I mean, — I cannot accept your conclusion. Listen to me a moment, and don't interrupt. I will acknowledge that I should like to make Gertrude Van Vleck my wife, but let us look at the matter from all points of view. In the first place, I have no means of knowing that she esteems me more than other men. I have grown distrustful, Richard, of my own impressions in a matter of this kind. Her cordiality toward me may mean anything or nothing.

But, after all, that is not the important point.
The fact is, my boy, that I have no right to
woo her. I have made a failure of life, for one
thing. Furthermore, I have been for some
years a determined foe to the institutions that
have surrounded her with wealth and luxury.
I am willing to acknowledge that I am not as
aggressive a radical as I was some time ago, but
that does not alter the fact that I have long
been an outspoken opponent of timocracy."

"Timocracy?" exclaimed Richard. "The
word sounds familiar, but my Greek is rusty.
What does it mean, John?"

Fenton looked at his friend suspiciously. For
an instant he had a feeling that Richard was
ridiculing him. But the earnest expression in
the youth's face reassured him.

"Timocracy, you remember, Richard, established a man's social and political status accord-
ing to the amount of grain he owned. We
have a timocracy in this country, in fact, if not
in theory. A man is known by the *companies*
he is in. But this is wandering a long way from
the point. The fact is, Richard, that I have

been under a tremendous temptation for the last few weeks, a temptation against which my better nature has been at war. What if I had given in to it, and had, let us say, won the hand of Gertrude Van Vleck? I could never make her happy. Ten years ago, perhaps, such a woman might have moulded me into something approaching an ideal husband. But time is tyrannical, Richard. It is too late now for me to ask of life the greatest blessing that it holds for man, a companionable wife. I cannot accept the sacrifice of youth, beauty, intellect, and affection on the altar of my selfishness. It wouldn't do, Richard. It wouldn't do at all. Let the dream pass! Come, boy, help me to be a man. Let us try London, Richard, and see if its fogs can't hide the foolish mirage our fevered brains have raised. You need heroic treatment as much as I do. From one standpoint, in fact, your case, Richard, is worse than mine. If you stay here you may bring misery to at least three people. If I remain, the worst I could do would be to make myself and one other unhappy. Mathematically you are more deserving of exile than I am."

"I tell you, John," exclaimed Richard, his eyes resting on his friend's face affectionately, "I tell you I don't want you to bring me in as an important factor in this matter. You are treating a great crisis in your life with more cold-blooded cynicism than I thought you retained. Don't you see that you may be doing Gertrude Van Vleck a great wrong? Don't you understand that you may be recklessly throwing away your chance of lifelong happiness? What have your years, or your past, or your theories got to do with the matter? The only question at issue in the whole affair is this: Does Gertrude Van Vleck love you? If she does, your sacrifice would be simply a cruelty. If she doesn't, your sacrifice wouldn't be a sacrifice. That sounds Irish, but it expresses my meaning.

> 'He either fears his fate too much,
>   Or his deserts are small,
> That dares not put it to the touch,
>   To gain or lose it all.'"

An amused smile played over Fenton's pale face.

"And what course of action do you advise, young hot-head?"

"There is only one thing for you to do, John. Go to Gertrude Van Vleck, and tell her that you love her. If she accepts you, that settles the problem before us. If she rejects you, we will go to London."

Fenton arose, and resumed his impatient march up and down the room.

"How impetuous youth is!" he remarked after a time. Then he halted; and, standing in front of Richard, looked down at the young man solemnly. "You know little of true love, Richard. It is based on unselfishness and is only true to itself when it remains worthy of its foundation. Listen, boy, and learn. If I propose to Gertrude Van Vleck, and she rejects me, I have subjected to a painful experience the woman I love. If she accepts me, the same result, emphasized, is reached; for I am not worthy of her, Richard. I could not make her happy. No, no; do not answer me. No man can tell another what is the right course in such an affair as this. I have confessed to

you more than I ever expected to reveal to
any one. I have fought my fight and won
my victory."

Fenton turned, and seated himself wearily.
"It has not been easy for me, Richard," he
continued after a long silence. "But let that
pass. If you really care for me, — and I feel
that you do, — you will never refer to the matter again. I have dreamed my dream, and
the awakening has come. I see clearly that
there is only one way for me to be true to
myself and just to others. I shall take that
way. And now, Richard, let us talk of our
plans. You have never been in London?"

Richard Stoughton's heart was heavy as he
talked with Fenton about their future. He
could not but admire the strength and nobility
of his friend's character; but there seemed to
be something left unsaid, some argument not
yet advanced, that might throw a different
light on the problem Fenton had weighed and
solved for himself. But Richard had learned
in the last few months that there was a stubbornness and pride in his companion's nature

that rendered opposition impossible after a
certain point had been reached.

Furthermore, he could not disguise from
himself that he was pleased at Fenton's decision in so far as it affected himself. Stoughton was a thorough modern in his ways of
looking at most subjects, and a few years of
experience and travel might easily make his
impressionable nature very broad in its tendencies. But there was an ancestral strain
of Puritanism in his make-up that still had a
strong influence on his ideas of life. Just what
his feelings toward Mrs. Percy-Bartlett were
he hardly knew ; but he realized that if he
continued to meet her on the footing that had
existed between them of late, he would in the
end lose sight of certain principles to which
he still fondly clung. He was old-fashioned
enough, as yet, to respect, in his cooler moments, the musty teachings that still prevail
in certain parts of New England regarding the
sacredness of another man's wife. He had
not yet grasped the comparatively modern discovery that to a bachelor all things are pure.

Then, again, with his fondness for Mrs. Percy-Bartlett was mingled an admiration for a vein of self-restraint that he felt certain existed in the foundation of her character.   He knew intuitively that if, by word or action, he overstepped certain well-defined boundaries, his intercourse with her would come to an abrupt and unpleasant end.

That Mrs. Percy-Bartlett was not especially fond of her husband he felt convinced, not by any word of hers, but from the indefinable but overwhelming testimony of airy nothings. That she had grown to care for him, Richard Stoughton, a youth who had brought something into her life the lack of which she had long felt, he could well imagine — without, perhaps, a too excessive egotism.   But from whatever point of view he considered the matter, the more it seemed to him best that the ocean should roll between them for a time.   Richard Stoughton, as the reader has long since observed, was a youth extremely sensitive to his surroundings.   The decision he had come to might never have been reached in the Percy-

Bartletts' music-room.   In Fenton's parlor, and
in the presence of a man who had made, in
Richard's sight, a great renunciation, it was
not so hard to live up to his highest ideals.

"And so," said Fenton as he arose to bid
his guest good-night, "and so, Richard, our
problems are solved at last.   Come to my room
at three o'clock on Monday and we will go
up and have a talk with Mr. Robinson.   Good-
night, my boy, and good luck.   I have much
to thank you for, Richard — but never mind
about it now.   Good-night."

CHAPTER XXII.

THE Percy-Bartletts were dining with Gertrude Van Vleck and her father. Cornelius Van Vleck was a man sixty years of age, whose life had been spent, for the most part, in maintaining the traditions of his family. As the Van Vlecks had been prominent in the city since the year 1636, the number of these traditions that he had been called upon to cherish rendered his task no sinecure.

Cornelius Van Vleck had good reason to be proud of his ancestors. They had possessed a combination of foresight and conservatism that had conferred on their posterity the blanket-blessing of vast wealth. The man who is a landed proprietor on Manhattan Island need never fear want. Banks may fail, the credit of the country may be threatened, railroads may dodge their dividends, and hard times may cast their shadow over a long-suffering

people, but the New York landlord is in-
trenched behind a financial Gibraltar.   How is
he to blame if his ancestors were thrifty and
far-seeing ?   Render to Cæsar the things that
are Cæsar's, ye grumbling and restless tenants,
and accept the world as you find it.   Cornelius
Van Vleck could no more help being rich than
you can avoid being poor.   Wherever the blame
may lie for the inequalities that exist in the
distribution of wealth, surely Cornelius Van
Vleck cannot be held responsible.   He is as
much the victim of a system as you are.   But
he bears his burden without a protest.   Never
during his long life as a man of great financial
and social importance has Cornelius Van Vleck
been heard to reproach his ancestors for the
load of responsibility that they placed upon his
shoulders.   He has lived up to his position in
the community with an almost heroic devotion
to his lofty duties ; and in his old age he is
still inspired by that fine old motto of *noblesse
oblige.*

One of the hereditary obligations to which
he has always conformed, for the honor of his

forefathers and his own satisfaction, consists in dining well. Cornelius Van Vleck has the reputation of giving the most artistic dinners in the city. But he never casts pearls before swine. His guests must be worthy of his *chef*. The hospitable but somewhat testy old gentleman demands from those who sit at his board an appreciation as keen as his own of the gastronomic excellence of the entertainment provided. It is for this reason that he always enjoys having the Percy-Bartletts at his table. Whether Mrs. Percy-Bartlett fully appreciates the delicate lights and shades of the epicurean masterpieces produced by the Van Vlecks' *chef*, the host has never been quite certain. But he has no doubt of Mr. Percy-Bartlett's ability to understand and rejoice in the fine touches that the artist below stairs so deftly makes.

"I have my doubts, my friend," he is saying to Percy-Bartlett, as they puff their cigars and sip a liqueur after the ladies have retired to the drawing-room, "I have my doubts that a woman can ever become a thoroughly equipped *connoisseuse* at the dinner-table. I know that there is no line of endeavor in which the new woman does not feel competent to shine; but," and here the old gentleman waved his liqueur-glass at Percy-Bartlett with a stately and hospitable gesture, "but they haven't that delicate sense of taste, that sensitiveness to the most refined and elusive flavors that we men possess. Do you know, there are some dishes that I can't make Gertrude eat at all! Just imagine, sir, a woman, an intellectual woman, who takes pride in shocking her old father with her advanced ideas and theories, and who has had every advantage of travel and instruction, who absolutely refuses to eat terrapin in any form. How, sir, can woman expect us to acknowledge her equality when she boldly admits that she doesn't like terrapin?"

Percy-Bartlett smiled; but his eyes were restless, his face pale, and his manner that of a man who is making an effort to be sociable against his inclinations.

"I think, Mr. Van Vleck," he replied, "that you and I are in close sympathy regarding the absurd pretensions made by women to-day.

Do you know, sir, I have grown very weary of the whole thing. There is a restlessness, a pushing, discontented, crude, and unfeminine spirit abroad among the women of our set that has actually had a crushing effect upon me. I think that it is responsible for the constantly recurring fits of the blues that have bothered me so much of late."

Cornelius Van Vleck, whose heavy but not unsymmetrical features lacked mobility, gazed at his guest with some concern in his bluish-gray eyes.

"You aren't looking quite fit, young man, that's a fact. Take some of that brandy. It's something very fine, I assure you. By the way, why don't you knock off a bit, and run over to the other side with us? Gertrude and I are going over at once. She needs a change, a great change. There's something wrong with the girl. She has grown morbid and flighty, sir. I can't understand it — unless these new ideas that are floating around have struck in. She has been asking me some very embarrassing questions of late, sir, some very embarrassing questions. I even suspect that Gertrude has been visiting some of my tenants on the East Side, and distributing alms. As if organized charities were not sufficient to relieve the distress in the city! I have remonstrated with her, sir; but what can you do with a woman to-day? Whose authority do they respect, sir? A father's? a husband's?"

Percy-Bartlett sipped his brandy nervously, while a slight flush arose to his pallid cheeks.

"I thoroughly sympathize with you, Mr. Van Vleck. We are almost powerless to check this rebellious spirit. There is a limit, of course, to protest beyond which a gentleman cannot go. I fully realize that. There have been many things to disturb us of late; we, I mean, who cling to the old ideas and the best traditions of our set. And, do you know, I hold the newspapers responsible for a good deal of the harm that has been done."

"You are right, Percy-Bartlett! you are right!" cried his host with more animation than he usually displayed. "There have been those among us who seemed to actually crave notoriety. It has been shocking — shocking! I really don't know what we're coming to. Do you know, I gave a small dinner-party last night, — twelve at the table, you know, — and, will you believe me, a reporter came to the house and asked for a list of my guests. That's a straw that shows which way the wind blows. When I was young, sir, a man could dine at home without awakening the curiosity of the public. But, tell me, aren't you well? You look very pale. I am worried about you, my friend."

Percy-Bartlett was leaning back in his chair, a gray pallor on his face, and his lips almost colorless. Leaning forward with an effort, he swallowed the remaining drops of brandy in his glass.

"It is nothing, Mr. Van Vleck," he said, after a moment's silence; "I have been doing too much work and worrying of late. I really believe I need a vacation."

"You do indeed, sir," remarked his host emphatically. "Come, young man, listen to reason. The one great privilege that wealth grants is that it gives us our freedom. Come over to London with us. We sail Wednesday morning. Drop your work right here and take a rest. If you don't, you'll break down, Percy-Bartlett, and all the king's horses and all the king's men won't be able to pull you together again."

Percy-Bartlett looked at his elderly companion gratefully. It was a novel and welcome sensation to have some one take an interest in his welfare. There was silence for a time. Then he said, as he arose slowly, as though his head felt giddy, —

"Perhaps you are right, Mr. Van Vleck. Come into the drawing-room with me. I'll ask Harriet what she thinks of the scheme."

CHAPTER XXIII.

"Even if it turns out happily, Harriet, I will always feel that she did an unwomanly thing."

Mrs. Percy-Bartlett and Gertrude Van Vleck were seated *en tête-à-tête* in the drawing-room, talking of a quiet wedding that had taken place recently in the inner circle. This matrimonial event had possessed peculiar features. It was rumored, on evidence more conclusive than gossip often enjoys, that the bride had done the larger part of the wooing and had actually proposed to the man of her choice. What the circumstances were that had led to this reversal of ancient custom on the part of people to whom time-honored precedents are especially dear nobody but the high contracting parties knew; but it was well understood that the woman had taken the initiative, and had been successful in her egotistic match-making. There were a good many spinsters in society

who approved of her course, but Gertrude Van
Vleck was not among them.

"But," argued Mrs. Percy-Bartlett, "I
thought, Gertrude, that you were progressive.
You seem to accept many of the new ideas,
but reject others. I am sure I can't see why
she did an unwomanly thing. In these days
there is hardly anything that can be called
unwomanly — if it is done gracefully."

Gertrude smiled sadly as she looked into her
friend's sympathetic eyes. They both realized
that the problem they were discussing was not
an abstract question, but that, on the contrary,
it possessed a concrete and vital significance
for one of them.

"I'm afraid, Harriet," said Gertrude musingly, "that I cannot keep up with women who
are determined to be in the front ranks of the
new movement. I have too many conservative
characteristics in my make-up, inherited from
my father."

She looked about her with restless eyes, her
glance seeming to appeal to the spirit of the
room in which they sat for strength and com-

fort. There are many drawing-rooms in New York that combine luxury with taste. Not a few are actually regal in their magnificence. But a drawing-room that indicates ancestral glories, that seems to rejoice in the fact that it is the storehouse of patrician memories, is a rarity. The Van Vlecks' drawing-room was a shrine sacred to the cult of true American aristocracy. You might pooh-pooh the Van Vlecks' coat-of-arms, their family livery, or other outward manifestations of ancestral pride, but only an iconoclast deluded by delirium could enter that drawing-room without feeling the subtle influence that it exerted in opposition to the image-breakers of to-day.

Suddenly Mrs. Percy-Bartlett broke the silence that had followed Gertrude's last remark.

"You sail Wednesday. You do not expect to see him before you go?"

"No. Why should I? He will not come to me again."

"Tell me, Gertrude, how you know," said Mrs. Percy-Bartlett gently, taking the girl's cold hand in hers.

"It is hard to explain," remarked Gertrude wearily. "I understand him so well, Harriet. He is very proud, and has such queer ideas! He — he — don't think me awfully conceited, Harriet — he — I'm sure he likes me. But I never expect to see him again."

There was the suspicion of a sob in her voice. Mrs. Percy-Bartlett gazed earnestly into her friend's eyes.

"Tell me, Gertrude," she said beseechingly, "what has happened. You are concealing something from me."

"Nothing, truly," exclaimed Gertrude, a frank smile on her lips. "There has been absolutely nothing between Mr. Fenton and myself that you do not know about, Harriet."

"But why, my dear, do you say that you never expect to see him again? I can't understand it."

"I hardly know how to explain it to you, Harriet. I am not in the habit of placing too much confidence in intuition and inexplicable impressions, but I feel certain that he will never come to me again — unless I send for him."

Mrs. Percy-Bartlett was silent for a time. Things seemed so fatally wrong in the world at that moment. She felt confused, discontented, wholly unfit to give comfort or advice to her unhappy friend. And yet why should she not urge her to take a step that might lead to happiness? Why should pride and precedent be permitted to stand between John Fenton and Gertrude Van Vleck when the very spirit of the age was teaching men and women to be broad-minded and reasonable, and, perhaps, more natural? Impulsively she turned to Gertrude and bent very close to her.

"My dear girl, you are doing him and yourself a great wrong. You should write to him and ask him to come to you. It is the only way."

"And when he comes?" asked Gertrude in a whisper.

Mrs. Percy-Bartlett bent and kissed the pale cheek of the trembling girl.

"Tell him that you love him, Gertrude."

A flush overspread Gertrude's face and her

eyes flashed. She arose and looked down at her friend.

"I cannot, Harriet. When you put it into words, it scares me. It is horrible to talk of such a thing. I am sorry — so sorry, that you said it." She reseated herself and looked into the sad, brown eyes that gazed at her almost reproachfully.

"I know that you meant it for the best, Harriet, but it can never be. And, now, promise me that you will never refer to this again. You know my secret. Let us go on as though I had never told you."

They were silent for a time, their cold hands clasped in a contact that expressed more than words. After a time Gertrude spoke, —

"I am so sorry to go away from you just now, Harriet. I never needed you so much before."

Mrs. Percy-Bartlett sighed wearily.

"I am so tired, Gertrude. When you are gone I don't know what I shall do. Life is such a weird and wearisome affair. I am young, and the world has given me every-

thing that I ought to ask of it — but —
but " —

She hesitated. Gertrude bent toward her.

"I think I understand, my dear. I am so
sorry."

There was a note of sympathetic pity in
her voice that was sweet and soothing in
her hearer's ear. They were both tasting
the bitter cup that every man and woman
must sometime hold to the lips, and in the
moment of their sorrow their friendship for
each other became more precious than it
had ever been. It was hard to part at the
greatest crisis in their lives, to say farewell
when they needed from each other the inspiration that the closest intercourse could
give.

Cornelius Van Vleck and Percy-Bartlett entered the drawing-room.

"I have great news for you both," cried
the former as he came forward, his phleg-
matic face more animated than usual.

They looked up at him inquiringly.

"Your husband and I have a secret, Mrs.

Percy-Bartlett," he went on playfully. "Are you not curious to know what it is?"

"Of course I am, Mr. Van Vleck. Am I not a woman?"

The glimpse she caught of her husband's face startled her. There was an unnatural flush in his cheeks, and his eyes were feverishly bright.

"What is it, dear?" she exclaimed, rising and putting her hand on his arm. Percy-Bartlett smiled reassuringly.

"Nothing serious," he answered. "I disobeyed the doctor and smoked one of Mr. Van Vleck's cigars. Furthermore," and he looked at his host knowingly, "I fear that I am threatened with an attack of *mal-de-mer.*"

Gertrude Van Vleck sprang up in excitement.

"Do you mean it?" she cried. "O Harriet! don't you understand? You are going with us. Am I not right, papa?"

Cornelius Van Vleck smiled benignantly.

"I have become your husband's medical adviser," he remarked, turning to Mrs. Percy-

Bartlett, " and have ordered him to take a sea-voyage for his health."

"And you have agreed?" asked Mrs. Percy-Bartlett of her husband, her voice cold, almost harsh, from the excitement that she restrained.

" If you wish," he answered, seating himself wearily, and looking up at his wife with an affectionate gleam in his eyes.

"It is almost too good to be true," cried Gertrude Van Vleck, trying to meet Harriet's averted gaze. " I am so happy."

" Is it not charming, Gertrude?" said Mrs. Percy-Bartlett, seating herself by her husband's side and speaking with as much enthusiasm as she could summon to her aid. But she was not an actress, and to her husband and her confidante there seemed to be an unconvincing note in her voice, a suggestion that she was accepting the inevitable with a protest that vainly craved expression.

CHAPTER XXIV.

MRS. PERCY–BARTLETT was seated at the piano, idly striking chords that seemed to vibrate with the melancholy of her mood. It was Tuesday evening, and her husband had gone to his club to attend to several matters that required settlement before his departure. They were to sail for Europe early on the following morning, and Mrs. Percy-Bartlett's revery was one of mingled apprehension and regret. Her mind assured her that the exile before her was the best possible solution of a problem that had forced itself upon her; her heart revolted against the thought of a difficult but imperative step that she must take. She had sent a note that morning to Richard Stoughton, telling him that she was to leave for Europe on Wednesday and that she would be glad to see him in the evening, if he was at leisure. The messenger had returned with an answer to her note that had filled her with surprise and consternation.

"I will call this evening," Richard had written, "not to say adieu to you, but to bid us both *bon voyage*. I am overjoyed at the outlook."

What these enigmatical words meant she had been unable to determine. He seemed to imply that he, too, was to sail for Europe in the morning. If that were the case, she realized that she had a hard task before her. Her instinct told her that it would be fatally unwise for them to make the voyage together. In the first place, the presence of Richard Stoughton on the steamer would look very queer to Percy-Bartlett. Surely the increase of his jealousy was not the line of treatment likely to restore her husband to health. Furthermore, she longed for rest and peace. She had rebelled in her heart at first against the idea of running away from the one great pleasure of her life, the comradeship of Richard Stoughton ; but later on her mood had changed, and she had begun to take a melancholy satisfaction in the thought that if absence might mean pain and longing it would also beget its own anæsthetic.

And now she sat awaiting Richard's coming, her heart beating feverishly, her face pale and her eyes restless and brilliant. She had determined, if the worst came to the worst, that she would ask him to make a great sacrifice for her on the altar of friendship. She had not reached this decision without a struggle. It would be so pleasant to have him with her on the voyage! She had grown to take so much pleasure in his companionship that it seemed almost sacrilege to place any obstacle in the path of events that conspired to prolong their intimacy. And it was chance, not design, that was responsible for the fact — if it were a fact — that they were to sail for the Old World together. But Mrs. Percy-Bartlett was too clever a woman to allow the tempting fallacies that beset her mind to long have sway. She realized that it is very easy to find arguments to defend and justify almost any course of action ; but she still retained her confidence in that

vague, indefinable, but insistent guide that is
generally called conscience, and when she was
weary of inward debate she always fell back
on it for the final word, the motive-power that
should carry her in the right direction. In
this instance, conscience whispered to her that
either Richard Stoughton or herself must remain in New York when the Majestic left the
pier in the morning. That it would be well
nigh impossible for her to make a change in
her plans without undergoing many embarrassing questions from her husband, she well
knew. Her ultimate hope lay in Richard
Stoughton's unselfishness. If he cared for
her " in the right way," as she put it to herself, he would alter his movements for her
sake.

The portière was pushed back, and a servant
announced " Mr. Stoughton." Richard entered
the music-room, a flush of pleasure and excitement on his cheeks and the joy of youthful enthusiasm in his eyes.

As she gave him her hand it felt as cold
as marble in his grasp, and he saw that her

face was pale and her expression one of apprehension rather than delight.

"Something is worrying you," he said, as he seated himself where he could look into her face. "Did you not understand my note?"

She smiled sadly. "I fear that I did," she answered in a low voice. "You sail on the Majestic to-morrow morning?"

"Yes."

"I am very sorry," she faltered, feeling that it was harder to obey the voice of conscience than she had thought it would be.

The light in his face died out and he looked at her with mingled surprise and regret.

"I had thought," he said, almost bitterly, "that you would be pleased to have me for a fellow-traveller."

How could she explain to him her feelings in the matter? His very youth made it difficult. It would be so easy for him to misunderstand her. At that moment she felt that she was years older than this man whose birthday was in the same month as her own. And in his presence it was harder to make the sacrifice she had determined upon than it had appeared to be an hour before. She looked up at him shyly. His face had grown pale and the smile had died away from his lips. A woman never knows how much she really cares for a man until she is obliged to ask of him a great renunciation for her sake. It is in the nature of a generous and affectionate woman to confer favors, not to plead for them.

The silence in the room had grown embarrassing. She turned and almost impatiently struck a few sombre chords on the piano. She feared that he would see the tears that had gathered in her eyes.

Richard arose and walked to the farther end of the room, then turned and approached her. Her golden-brown hair, the whiteness of her neck, and the rounded outlines of her shoulders thrilled him with mingled delight and despair. He was vaguely conscious of the fact that this woman was asking of him a sacrifice that he would find it hard to make. He understood her well enough to realize that in his own inherent generosity she was placing a confidence that demanded on his part both reticence and renunciation. She had said that she was sorry that they were to be companions on an ocean voyage. Feverishly his mind endeavored to grasp the full significance of her words. He could not at that moment weigh them in all their bearings, but it was enough that she had expressed regret at the coincidence that had turned their faces toward Europe at the same moment. It would be cruel, unnecessary, to make her explain herself more fully. One thought overshadowed all others in his mind. If she did not care for him, — why should he mince words? — did not love him, she would not admit that she was sorry that he was to be by her side for so long a time. She had confessed to him that the shadow of self-distrust was on her soul. He could not ask for more. All men may be selfish, but at a great crisis there are those who can be chivalric.

Richard reseated himself and looked at her mournfully.

"You have a favor to ask of me," he ventured after a time.

She turned and glanced at him, with a gleam of merriment in her changeful eyes.

"You sometimes seem to me to have clairvoyant power," she remarked. "Yes, I have a request to make — but it seems so selfish of me! It is the hardest thing I ever had to do."

He arose and stood looking down into her face.

"Please don't feel that it is difficult," he said gently. "I think I know what you would ask. If you wish, I will put off my departure until Saturday. No, don't thank me. I shall find my reward in the thought that — that " —

He hesitated, and she raised her face until their eyes met. He bent toward her.

"In the thought that you may realize how hard it is for me to let you go."

He had taken both her hands, and the tears in her eyes made it well-nigh impossible for her to see how close his lips were to hers.

"You are a noble fellow," she whispered.

Richard was torn with the tempest of love and desperation that filled his soul. The incense of her hair, the warm caress of her breath as it touched his face, the sad, white misery of her trembling lips seemed to madden him. He hesitated an instant, while the spirits of light and darkness warred within him. Then a strange thing happened. He heard, as though the speaker stood close to his ear, the ringing voice of the preacher who had stirred his soul amid the solemn shadows of a church some weeks before, and it seemed to say: "Be true to your manhood; for the light that is within you is divine."

Richard turned on the instant, unconscious that his overwrought nerves had worked what seemed at the moment to be a miracle. White and trembling, he sank into the chair by the side of the sobbing woman, whose icy hand still rested wearily in his.

As he had turned, it had seemed to him that the portières at the end of the room were falling into place, as though they had been suddenly disturbed; but as he looked at them again, hanging heavy and quiet in the shadows, he felt that the fever that had caused him to hear a stranger's voice had cast its delirious witchery upon his vision. But the truth was that his ears had played him false, while his eyes had not.

CHAPTER XXV.

IN certain respects Percy-Bartlett was an ideal clubman. He was a member of several exclusive clubs, but he frequented only one. He took more interest in the welfare of this organization than he did in the growth of the West or the opening of Africa to civilization. Philanthropists might have called him narrow-minded. He would have been astonished at the accusation. He subscribed liberally to the fund of his church for foreign missions and had once helped to equip a Polar expedition. A man who could open his purse to enterprises of this character would never look upon himself as an individual restricted in his sympathies. Cannot a man be a broad-minded benefactor of his race without seeking the companionship of those beneath him in the social make-up? Percy-Bartlett never imagined for a moment that in confining his intercourse to those whom he considered his equals, he was putting himself out of touch with the age and world in which he lived. Theoretically, he acknowledged the brotherhood of man. Practically, he found satisfaction only in the companionship of men who were eligible to membership in his favorite club. He devoted a tithe of his fortune to charity; why should he not have the privilege of giving most of his time to clubdom? Percy-Bartlett, like a good many Americans, acknowledged the grandeur of the Declaration of Independence, but did not feel that that instrument had established a ritual.

It is said that a man cannot serve both God and Mammon. However this may be, — and there are clever individuals who seem to fight under both banners, — it is certain that it takes genius for a man to do his duty equally well to his club and to his home. Percy-Bartlett was not a genius. He was a thorough gentleman, of fair ability, who had found himself inclined, at one time, to sacrifice his club for the sake of his home. But, other things being equal,

a man, in the long run, will take the path in
which he finds the readiest and most pronounced sympathy. Percy-Bartlett was appreciated at his true worth at his club. He
realized vaguely that at his home he was in an
atmosphere that was not wholly congenial, and
that he did not hold the high place in the
bosom of his family that assures to a husband
the domestic felicity that is, in the end, fatal to
prominence in club life. A companionable
husband, like anything else worth having, is
the product of assiduous cultivation. The
converse is also true ; and a man cannot enjoy
the intercourse of a thoroughly congenial
woman unless he has the tact and perseverance
necessary to the production of this rare and
priceless blossom of the social flora. Marriage
is like a garden, in which two plants are set
aside to tend each other. If one of them is
neglectful of the task imposed upon it, they
both suffer equally ; and the garden in which
they have been placed grows narrow and dis-
tasteful in their sight. If you grasp the full
significance of this illustration, O gentle reader,

you will be able to understand why it is that in these progressive times not only married men but married women have their clubs. We all crave sympathy, and an outlet for the unrest that is in us. If we cannot find them at home, we must go to our club, where we may meet some one who understands us, and who will offer us a relief-pipe for the pent-up individuality that so sorely chafes us. And thus it is that both men and women need their clubs to-day. The end of the last century found the world emphasizing the brotherhood of man. The end of the present century is busy underscoring the sisterhood of woman. Is it strange that the last years of the eighteenth century were not more disturbing to the institution of marriage than are the closing days of the nine-teenth century? The only conclusion that seems deducible to the student of contemporary social unrest is that the millennium will not be reached until the problem of how to make a home a club is solved.

Percy-Bartlett was not especially happy, although such an admission was the last that he would willingly have made to himself. He had grown accustomed to deceiving himself into the belief that he thoroughly enjoyed life. Surely it had done much for him. He had wealth, position, friends, and a beautiful and accomplished wife. But slowly the fine flavor of existence had passed away, and sometimes the unwelcome thought would force itself upon him that he was a tired and lonely man. Never by word or look did he hint at this suspicion, even to his most intimate friends. They had noticed of late that he had lost his spirits and looked ill and weary; but he had spoken of his recurrent attacks of indigestion, and they had seen that he had become very abstemious in the use of alcohol and tobacco. That there was anything radically wrong with him neither he nor they suspected.

Percy-Bartlett was in a more cheerful mood than usual when he left his club on Tuesday evening at an earlier hour than was his wont to return home. The future looked brighter than it had appeared for some time past. He had placed his affairs in such shape that he could take a long vacation without worrying about the details of his personal interests. He walked rapidly down the avenue, anxious to have a long chat with his wife before retiring. They would be obliged to rise early in the morning to take the steamer, which left her pier at eleven o'clock.

There was a smile of contentment on his face as he thought that a change of scene and the excitement of travel might do much to draw his wife closer to him. She would have no time on the journey, he reflected, to become wholly absorbed in her musical pursuits. That he had grown jealous of Richard Stoughton he had never acknowledged to himself, but he had long resented the rivalry of his wife's piano, and he rejoiced at the fact that she could not take it with her.

Furthermore, he realized that his precarious health demanded from him a long rest and a thorough change of scene. He was not over-fond of travel, but in these days the possession of wealth insures to the tourist an amount of comfort that is almost equal to that obtained from his club. From all points of view, the immediate future looked bright to Percy-Bartlett as he slowly mounted the steps of his house, and puffing slightly from the exertion, quietly opened the hall-door with a night-key. He would come upon his wife quietly and enjoy the expression of surprise on her face at his early return. That there would be a warm welcome in her smile he hardly dared to hope. But it is very easy to fall into the habit of expecting from those we love the reflection of the mood that we happen to be in. That Percy-Bartlett had often been disappointed in obtaining from his wife the sympathy he craved had not made him despair of sometime winning from her the response to his affection that he knew she had the power to give.

The moment seemed to him to be favorable for breaking down the barriers that had so long appeared to separate him from his wife. He would find her in the music-room. Diplomate that he was, he would ask her to sing one or two of her own songs to him, and then he would tell her of the outlines of their journey that he had prepared, and would make whatever changes in the itinerary that she suggested. He could see her, in imagination, closing her piano for the last time, and turning to him with a bright smile on her face when she had locked the instrument and put the key in her pocket.

His heart beat with stifling rapidity as he quietly entered the drawing-room. He smiled as the thought flashed through his mind that he was more in the mood of a young lover, staking his life's happiness on a few burning words, than in that of a middle-aged husband about to discuss the prosaic details of a European trip with his wife.

The drawing-room was dimly lighted, and the portières at the entrance to the music-room were closely drawn. He approached them noiselessly, somewhat surprised that his rival, the piano, was not taking advantage of his absence to strengthen its hold upon his wife.

Gently he laid his trembling hand upon the heavy hangings, and looked into the music-room. Then he dropped the portière and turned away, his face ghastly in its pallor, and his eyes wild with sudden pain. He staggered forward across the drawing-room, making an heroic effort to avoid stumbling against the furniture. Strangely enough, the one overpowering fear that possessed him at the moment was that, by some accident, he should make his presence known in the music-room. He looked, as he actually skulked toward the hall, like a man who had committed some awful crime, and who was making a desperate effort to avoid detection. Great beads of perspiration had broken out upon his brow. His face was drawn and set, and his lips were pressed against his teeth in a way that gave his countenance an expression of ghastly mirth.

The dread that beset him was that in the hall he would attract the attention of one of the servants. Trembling with cold, he crept into his overcoat and tip-toed to the door. All was silent in the house. Out into the night he stole, glancing furtively up and down the avenue like one who dreads detection. He reeled with dizziness as he reached the sidewalk and leaned for a moment against a railing. The night air seemed to revive him after a time; for pulling himself together with a mighty effort, he moved on toward his club like one who walks in sleep and flees from the phantoms of his dream.

CHAPTER XXVI.

"IT is hard, Gertrude; very hard! But I must be in London a week from to-day."

Gertrude Van Vleck looked up at her father as he uttered these words, and her face grew a shade paler, while the tears started to her eyes. She was clad in a travelling costume that was extremely becoming to her tall and graceful figure. In her hand she held an almost unde-cipherable scrawl. It was from Mrs. Percy-Bartlett, and ran as follows:—

"MY DEAR GERTRUDE,—Perhaps you have already heard the awful news. My husband died suddenly at the Union Club last night. I am so utterly stunned that I cannot write coherently, but one insistent thought is with me at this sad time. You must not change your plans on my account. I long for you at this moment with my whole heart, but my selfishness must have no weight with you. If you really wish it, I will join you in London soon; but I can make no special arrangements just now.

I will write to you or send you a cable message as soon as I have the strength and opportunity to think of the future."

" Listen, Gertrude," continued Mr. Van Vleck, almost sternly, " We have no time to lose. Don't think me heartless, my child ; but I must be in London on the date I have set, for many reasons that would not interest you. Sit down and write to Mrs. Percy-Bartlett at once. Tell her that we will wait for her in London, and take her to the Continent with us. I absolutely cannot wait over a steamer at this time. Poor little woman, I am sorry that there is no other way."

With a heavy heart Gertrude Van Vleck penned a note — how inadequate, almost heartless, it appeared to her as she re-read it — and despatched it by a messenger to Mrs. Percy-Bartlett. The generous, affectionate heart of the girl rebelled against the necessity that compelled her to take this course ; but there seemed to be, at the moment, no alternative.

Gertrude had had but little personal contact with that mysterious thing we call death.

The suddenness of her friend's bereavement appalled her. There comes a time in every one's experience, early or late, when the insignificance of one human life in the make-up of the illimitable universe is emphasized with a stunning force that leaves us wiser, perhaps, but infinitely more sad. Gertrude Van Vleck had thought much about the strange problems that the life of the world presents, but the final and most significant riddle that haunts the mind of man, the awful question that death asks, had never touched her deeply. But now it had come to her in a new guise, and she felt crushed and hopeless with the pitiless suddenness of the shock.

The drive to the steamer seemed almost interminable. The noises of the streets, the disjointed exclamations of her father, the feverish throbbing in her head, caused Gertrude the most acute suffering. The bustle and excitement at the pier aggravated the restlessness and discontent that made her whole being ache. There seemed to be something childish in the vivacity of the men and women around her, who came and went, laughed and cried, were silent or loquacious, as if a voyage across the Atlantic were a thing of great moment. What was it compared with that mysterious journey into the unknown that we must all take to-day, or to-morrow, or a few years hence?

It was not until the steamer was well down the bay, and the cool, salt breeze that swept the decks had begun to bring the color back to Gertrude's cheeks, that she was able to throw off the dreary thoughts that oppressed her. And even then it was not with a cheerful gleam in her eyes that she gazed out upon the throbbing sea. Her heart cried out in revolt against the fate that had followed her. She was leaving behind her all that had made life interesting of late. The only woman she really cared for, and the only man she had ever felt that she could love, were going out of her life, as the great city sank toward the horizon in the west. It was very hard. She gazed down upon the waters rushing backward in her sight, while the hot tears filled her eyes, and the sea-breeze kissed them cold against her cheek.

"This is a weird and inexplicable world," she heard a voice that thrilled her with mingled amazement and joy saying at her side. She started, for the words seemed to give expression to her very thought, and turning, she beheld John Fenton, his face reflecting the wonder and delight that filled her soul. Her hand trembled as she placed it in his for a moment.

"I am so glad to see you," she said simply, but her voice trembled with the nervous reaction that affected her. "I — I — did not know that you were going abroad."

John Fenton kept her cold hand in his much longer than perfect etiquette warranted. Words come less readily to a man than to a woman at a great and unexpected crisis, and he was silent for some time. Finally he said, as he leaned against the rail and looked at her white face, that still bore traces of her despairing mood, —

"What is to be, will be. Tell me, are you a fatalist?"

"I hardly know," she answered. "Everything seems inexplicable and unnatural to me at this moment. You have heard that Percy-Bartlett is dead?"

"Yes," answered Fenton, gazing seaward for a moment. "I received a note from Richard Stoughton this morning. He was coming with me, you know. He has postponed the voyage for a week or so."

Gertrude's blue eyes looked into his questioningly.

"He was there last evening?" she asked.

"Yes. He was just leaving when Mrs. Percy-Bartlett received a note from Buchanan Budd saying that her husband had died suddenly at the club."

"I am very glad that Mr. Stoughton did not sail," she said, more to herself than to Fenton. It was strange how much the salt air had done to restore the color to her face and the light of contentment to her eyes. "She — that is Mrs. Percy-Bartlett, you know — is coming over to us at once."

There was silence for a time. As they looked down at the surging waters, the strange coincidence that had thrown them together

again seemed to them both to take on a super-
natural character.

"You were going away without bidding me
good-by," she said in a low voice.   Her eyes
met his reproachfully.

"You do me an injustice," he returned.   "I
wrote to you this morning."

She turned from him, and her eyes sought
the horizon.   She felt that his words had
placed her in an embarrassing position.   She
could not ask him what his letter said; but
she longed to know.

They stood without speaking for some time.
He was gazing at her clear-cut profile, and, as
he looked, the scruples that had led him to
make a great renunciation for her sake seemed
to him at that moment to be strained and
illogical.   Had he not made every sacrifice on
the altar of his Quixotic creed?   And had not
fate rendered his efforts futile?   Surely he
and Gertrude Van Vleck would not be standing together on the deck of an ocean steamer,
outward bound, if the stars in their courses
had not ordained that he should tell her what
was in his heart.

"I wish," he said at length, "that you would do me a favor."

She turned to him with a puzzled smile on her face.

"Promise me," he continued earnestly, "that, if the letter I sent to you this morning ever comes to your hand, you will destroy it unopened."

The smile died away from her face. He saw that he had placed himself in the position of being misunderstood. What could he do but explain himself? His face was pale with emotion, and he grasped the rail nervously.

"Gertrude," he said in a low voice, vibrant with suppressed passion, "Gertrude, I love you! Tell me, will you — can you give me hope?"

She was gazing seaward, with eyes that were moist with the tears of happiness.

Presently he felt a cold, trembling hand in his and the sun on the instant broke through the clouds and kissed the smiling sea, as their grasp grew firm with the fervor of their love.

THE END.

www.ingramcontent.com/pod-product-compliance
Lightning Source LLC
Chambersburg PA
CBHW030800020726
47499CB00006B/1709